In der Cornelsen Lernen App findest du viele Angebote für dieses Buch.

Achte in deinem Buch auf diese Zeichen:

- ▶ Hilfe — Hole dir in der App **Hilfe** für eine Aufgabe.
- ▶ Quiz — Mache das **Quiz** in der App. Finde heraus, was du schon kannst.
- ▶ Audio 33 — Höre das **Audio** in der App.
- ▶ Video 2 — Sieh das **Video** in der App an.

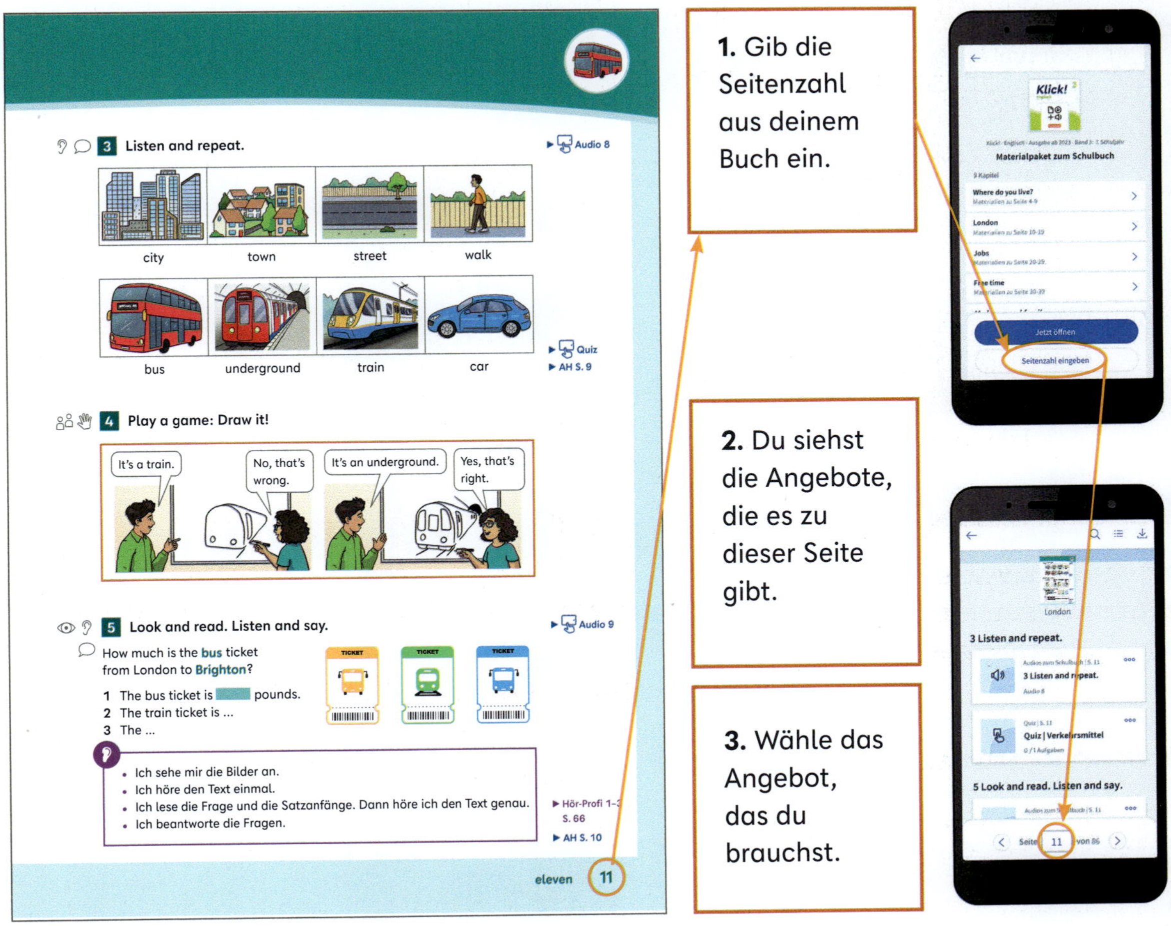

3

Klick!

Englisch

Erarbeitet von
Dr. Martina Koch
Berit Rudolph

In der **Cornelsen Lernen App** findest du passend zu deinem Englischbuch

- Audios
- Videos
- digitale Hilfen
- interaktive Elemente

Cornelsen

Klick!

Englisch 3

Ab Jahrgangsstufe 7

Erarbeitet von
Dr. Martina Koch, Nürnberg
Berit Rudolph, Lüneburg
sowie Zoe Thorne, Haywards Heath (Song)
und Miriam Güthler, Nürnberg (Quizzes)

In Zusammenarbeit mit der Englischredaktion
Klaus Unger (Projektleitung), Anne Linder (verantwortliche Redakteurin), Josephine Bienert-Köhler, Brianna Gorman, Chelsea Ledvinka-Heß, Denise Wendler sowie Georg Raspe, Düsseldorf (Wörterliste)

Beratende Mitwirkung
Stella Halank, Berlin; Matthias Schwarz, Mannheim; Petra Spengler, Dortmund; Gabriela Staňka, München; Amke Wolbert, Mannheim

Layoutkonzept
Klein & Halm, Berlin

Umschlaggestaltung
Anja Rosendahl, Berlin

Layout und technische Umsetzung
Klein & Halm, Berlin

Illustrationen
Joseph Wilkins sowie Carl Pearce (Cartoons), Beehive Illustration Agency, Cirencester, England; Nils Fliegner, Hamburg (Umschlag)

Fotos der Lehrwerkskinder
Chocolate Films, London sowie
Anja Poehlmann, Brighton (Lily)

Druck
Mohn Media Mohndruck, Gütersloh

PEFC
PEFC/04-31-1033

PEFC-zertifiziert
Dieses Produkt stammt aus nachhaltig bewirtschafteten Wäldern und kontrollierten Quellen
www.pefc.de

www.cornelsen.de

Soweit in diesem Lehrwerk Personen fotografisch abgebildet sind und ihnen von der Redaktion fiktive Namen, Berufe, Dialoge und Ähnliches zugeordnet oder diese Personen in bestimmte Kontexte gesetzt werden, dienen diese Zuordnungen und Darstellungen ausschließlich der Veranschaulichung und dem besseren Verständnis des Buchinhaltes.
Die enthaltenen Links verweisen auf digitale Inhalte, die der Verlag bei verlagsseitigen Angeboten in eigener Verantwortung zur Verfügung stellt. Links auf Angebote Dritter wurden nach den gleichen Qualitätskriterien wie die verlagsseitigen Angebote ausgewählt und bei Erstellung des Lernmittels sorgfältig geprüft. Für spätere Änderungen der verknüpften Inhalte kann keine Verantwortung übernommen werden.
Die Cornelsen Lernen App ist eine fakultative Ergänzung zu Klick!. Sie unterliegt nicht der Genehmigungspflicht.
Dieses Werk berücksichtigt die Regeln der reformierten Rechtschreibung und Zeichensetzung.

1. Auflage, 1. Druck 2025

Alle Drucke dieser Auflage sind inhaltlich unverändert und können im Unterricht nebeneinander verwendet werden.

ISBN 978-3-0603-6721-4

Jetzt mit barrierefreiem Farbkonzept
Mehr Informationen auf *cornelsen.de/bf*

Inhaltsverzeichnis

Where do you live? 4

London 10

Jobs 20

Free time 30

Digital life 40

Friends 50

Around the year 60

Meine Strategien: Hören, Sprechen, Lesen, Schreiben 66

Wörterliste 70

Let's talk: Classroom English 81

Numbers 83

Quellenverzeichnis 84

Karte: Europa 86

Karte: Vereinigtes Königreich von Großbritannien und Nordirland; Republik Irland U3

Aufgaben zur Text- und Medienkompetenz befinden sich auf diesen Seiten: 7, 8, 13, 15, 16-17, 19, 25, 26, 27, 33, 35, 36, 37, 39, 45, 46, 47, 49, 53, 55, 56, 57, 59, 61, 62, 63, 64.

Where do you live?

1

street art in London (England)

2

a football stadium in Manchester (England)

3

the castle in Inverness (Scotland)

4

the beach in Llandudno (Wales)

1 Look and find ...

- the graffiti
- the skateboard
- the big windows
- the beach
- the red and white chairs
- ...

2 Read. Listen and say.

▶ Audio 1

1 London is a ____ city in England.
2 Manchester has ____ big football clubs.
3 Inverness is not so ____.
4 You can eat ____ in Llandudno.

Finde auf der **Landkarte** hinten im Buch:
- die Landesteile von Großbritannien **England**, **Scotland**, **Wales**
- die Städte **London**, **Manchester**, **Inverness**, **Llandudno**.

▶ Karte: United Kingdom

3 Listen to Lily, Omar, Dylan and Grace. Answer.

▶ Audio 2

- Who lives in Manchester?
- Where is Inverness?

▶ Quiz
▶ AH S. 3 Nr. 1

4 Listen to Omar and Dylan. They are at a summer camp.

▶ Audio 3

5 Now you: Ask and answer. Use a dialogue card.

Hi, I'm **Lisa**. What's your name?
– My name is ___.
Nice to meet you, **Lisa**.

I live in **London**. Where do you live?
– I live in ___.
That's in ___.

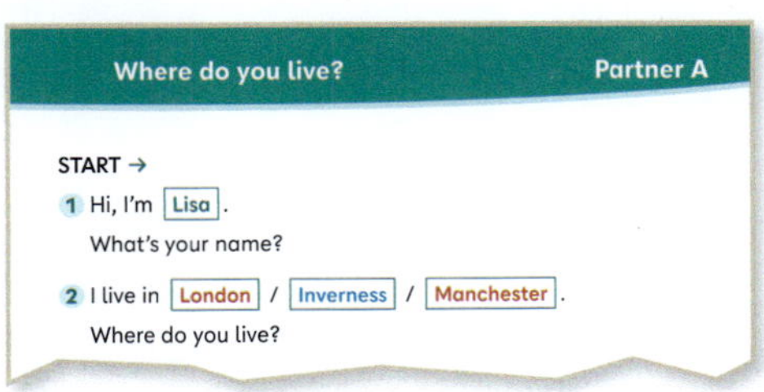
Where do you live? Partner A

START →
1 Hi, I'm Lisa.
What's your name?
2 I live in London / Inverness / Manchester.
Where do you live?

▶ AH Dialogkarte
▶ Quiz
▶ AH S. 3 Nr. 2

Where do you live?

1 **a) Listen to Lily, Dylan, Omar and Grace.** ▶ Audio 4

b) Now you: Ask and answer.

What **sports** do you like?
– I like **football** and **swimming**.

→

sports	food	music	?
darts • running • ?	pasta • hamburgers • ?	pop music • BTS • ?	?

▶ Hilfe

▶ Quiz
▶ AH S. 4

2 **a) Listen to Omar and Dylan.** ▶ Audio 5

b) Now you: Look. Ask and answer.

When do we meet for **breakfast**?
– We meet at **9 o'clock**.

	Monday	Tuesday	Wednesday
9.00		breakfast	
10.00	art	gardening	cleaning
12.30		lunch	
2.00	sports	walking	cycling
6.00		dinner	
7.30	dancing	games	films

▶ Quiz
▶ AH S. 5

3 a) Cartoon: Listen and read along.

▶ Audio 6

b) Read and answer.

1 What is Lily good at? What is Omar good at?
2 Who is happy 🙂? Who is sad 😢?

Time to say goodbye

It's Friday. It's the last day of summer camp. Everybody meets at the beach.

4 Now you: Talk in class.

What do you do with your friends in summer?

→

We	meet go play ?	at the skatepark. to the beach. table tennis. ?

▶ Hilfe

▶ AH S. 6

Great Britain and the United Kingdom

1 Look and find …

- the flags of Northern Ireland, Scotland, England and Wales.

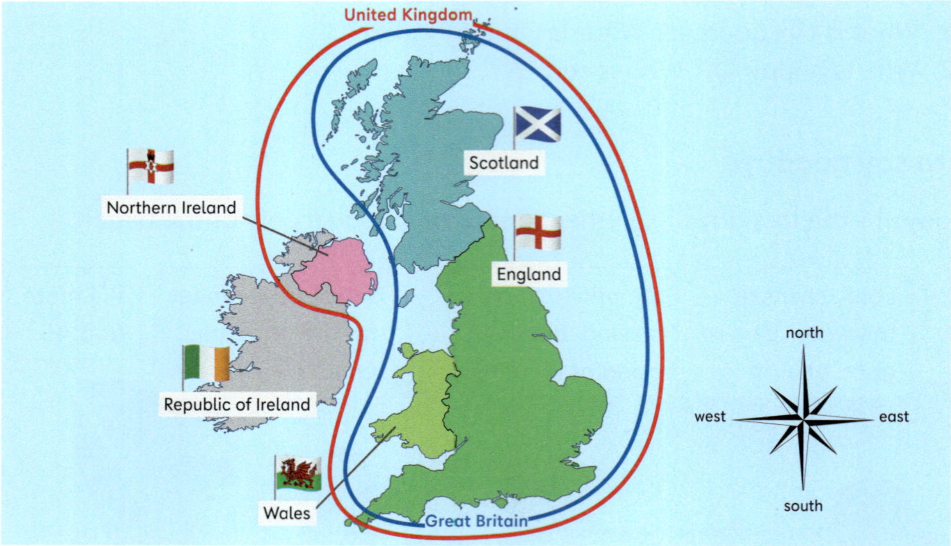

2 Life in Britain

Die Insel **Großbritannien** *(Great Britain)* liegt im Nordwesten von Europa. Die Insel Großbritannien besteht aus England, Schottland und Wales. Die Insel **Irland** liegt im Westen von Großbritannien. Auf der Insel Irland liegen Nordirland und die Republik Irland. Nordirland gehört zum **Vereinigten Königreich**. Die Republik Irland ist ein eigenständiger Staat. Die genaue Bezeichnung für den britischen Staat ist:
das Vereinigte Königreich von Großbritannien und Nordirland
(the United Kingdom of Great Britain and Northern Ireland).

- Gehe zur **Landkarte** hinten im Buch und finde:
  - die Hauptstadt der Republik Irland
  - die 4 Landesteile des Vereinigten Königreichs
  - die Hauptstädte der 4 Landesteile.
- In Deutschland gibt es 16 Bundesländer. Welche kennst du?

▶ Karte: United Kingdom

3 Watch the video. It's about the United Kingdom.

Where would you like to go?
– I'd like to go to Scotland.

▶ Video 1

▶ AH S. 7

New words and phrases

Read and say.

▶ Hilfe

Englisch lernen mit der App

- Lerne nicht länger als 10 Minuten am Stück.
- Lerne nur 3–5 Wörter oder Sätze auf einmal.
  1. Lies das englische Wort, dann die deutsche Bedeutung. Höre beides in der App an. Sprich leise mit.
  2. Sage das englische Wort oder den Satz.
  3. Höre das englische Wort oder den Satz.
  4. Sage die deutsche Bedeutung.
  5. Höre die deutsche Bedeutung.

So sagst du, wie du heißt und wo du wohnst:

What's your name?	Wie heißt du?
My name is Omar. / I'm Omar.	Ich heiße Omar. / Ich bin Omar.
Where do you live?	Wo wohnst du? / Wo lebst du?
I live in Manchester.	Ich wohne / lebe in Manchester.
That's in England.	Das ist in England.

So sagst du, welche Sportarten, welche Musik, ... du magst:

What sports do you like?	Welche Sportarten magst du?
I like running and football.	Ich mag Laufen und Fußball.

So sagst du, wann ihr euch (nach Plan) trefft:

When do we meet for lunch?	Wann treffen wir uns zum Mittagessen?
We meet at 12 o'clock.	Wir treffen uns um 12 Uhr.

▶ AH S. 8

London

1 Look and say.

I can see **Lily**.
There is **a takeaway**.
There are **two blue bikes**.

→
- a park
- an orange T-shirt
- a dog
- some apples
- ?

2 Read. Listen and answer.

▶ Audio 7

1 Where does Lily live? – She lives in ______.
2 What does Lily like about London? – She likes her new ______ and her new ______.
3 How does Lily feel? – She feels ______ and ______.

3 Listen and repeat.

▶ Audio 8

city	town	street	walk

bus	underground	train	car

▶ Quiz
▶ AH S. 9

4 Play a game: Draw it!

5 Look and read. Listen and say.

▶ Audio 9

How much is the **bus** ticket from London to **Brighton**?

1 The bus ticket is ______ pounds.
2 The train ticket is ...
3 The ...

- Ich sehe mir die Bilder an.
- Ich höre den Text einmal.
- Ich lese die Frage und die Satzanfänge. Dann höre ich den Text genau.
- Ich beantworte die Fragen.

▶ Hör-Profi 1–3 S. 66
▶ AH S. 10

London

1 a) Listen to Lily and Pearl.

▶ Audio 10

b) Now you: Ask and answer.

How do you get to school?

- I walk there.
- I get there by ______.

▶ AH S. 11

2 Listen. Now you: Ask and answer in class.

▶ Audio 11

→

- the cinema
- the park
- the youth centre
- the sports field
- the swimming pool
- the gaming shop
- ?

▶ Quiz
▶ AH S. 12

3 Look at the photos. Answer in German.

Worum geht es in dem Text?

The tube: We don't say "underground" in London. We say "the tube".

Bus: In London, get around by bus. It's great! You can see the city.

Bike: Do you like cycling? You can get around by bike too!

Walk: London is big, but you can walk too. There are lots of small and quiet streets in the city centre.

⚠ In Britan, look right first, then look left!

4 a) Read the text in 3 and listen. Find the answers 1–4.

▶ Audio 12

1 "The tube" is the ______ in London.
2 Get around by ______ and see the city.
3 Do you like cycling? Get around by ______.
4 In the city centre, you can ______ too.

Notizen machen
- Schreibe je ein Wort für die Lücken 1–4 auf.
- Überprüfe deine Notizen.
- Schreibe ganze Sätze in dein Heft.

b) Take notes. Check your notes.

▶ Hilfe

c) Write sentences 1–4 in your exercise book. Check your sentences.

▶ AH S. 13

London

1 Listen and repeat.

▶ Audio 13

see
sights

walk across
a bridge

visit
a museum

buy
a souvenir

▶ Quiz
▶ AH S. 14

2 a) Listen to Dylan and Lily.

▶ Audio 14

b) Now you: Make notes and talk.

Think. → Pair. → Share.

What can you do in your town?

- You can see ____.
- You can visit ____.
- You can buy ____.

☆
- You can walk across ____.
- You can go to ____.

▶ Hilfe

!
So benutzt du die Artikel ***the*** und ***a***:
a *museum* (**ein** Museum)
the *British Museum* (**das** Britische Museum)

▶ Quiz
▶ AH S. 15

3 Cartoon: Look, listen and read along.

▶ Audio 15

- Where is Lily at 3.45? Where is she at 4.15?
- Where is Lily at 4.30? And where is Pearl?

Where is Lily?

4 Listen to Lily and the German tourist. Answer in German.

▶ Audio 16

1 *Wohin möchte die Touristin fahren?*
2 *Welches Verkehrsmittel soll sie nehmen?*
3 *Wie viel kostet die Fahrkarte?*

▶ AH S. 16

London sights

www.studentblogs.example.com/new_in_london

New in London
I live in London.
It's a great city!
There are lots of great places and sights!

My favourite sight is the **London Eye**.
You can see the city from the London Eye.
A ticket is £22. ☹
My tip: Go there with your school class.
The ticket for students is £9.95. ☺
You can get there by tube or bus.

the London Eye

Lots of parks in London are free.
My favourite park is **St James's Park**.
You can chill and watch animals there.
You can get there by bus or tube.

St James's Park

Camden Market is a great place too.
You can buy cool clothes in the shops.
You can eat good food too.
You can get there by bus, tube or train.

Camden Market

The **British Museum** is so exciting.
You can see lots of cool things there.
The British Museum is free. That's great! ☺
You can get there by bus or tube.

the British Museum

Watch my video about London.

Grace635
Great video! ☺

O-Man
Manchester has lots of sights too. But London is so exciting!

1 **a) Look at Lily's blog. Answer in German.**

Worum geht es in Lilys Blog?

b) Read the blog and listen. Pick a sight: the London Eye, St James's Park or the British Museum.

► Audio 17

1 How do you get there?
2 What can you see or do there?
3 How much is a ticket?

	my sight:
1 get there	
2 what to do	
3 how much	

c) Find the answers 1–3. Take notes about your sight.

d) Talk to a partner.

2 **Watch Lily's video about London.**

► Video 2

1 How do you get to Buckingham Palace?
2 What can you do at Tower Bridge?
3 How much is a ticket for Madame Tussauds?

3 **Life in Britain**

London ist die Hauptstadt von England und dem Vereinigten Königreich *(United Kingdom)*. Etwa 10 Millionen Menschen leben in London. Etwa 20 Millionen Menschen besuchen London jedes Jahr. In London gibt es viele Sehenswürdigkeiten. Manche kosten Eintritt, manche sind kostenlos.

- Was würdest du in London unternehmen?
- Stell dir vor, Jugendliche aus einem anderen Land besuchen deine Stadt. Was würdest du mit ihnen unternehmen?

► AH S. 17

4 **Write about your town.**

I live in **Kirchheim**.
Kirchheim is a **nice town**.
You can visit the **Neckartor**.
You can go to the **skatepark**.

Einen Post über die eigene Stadt schreiben

- Was kann man in deiner Stadt unternehmen?
- Welche Sehenswürdigkeiten gibt es?

New words and phrases

Read and say.

▶ Hilfe
▶ AH Bildkarten

Englisch lernen mit den Bild-Wort-Karten
- Sieh das Bild an und sage das englische Wort.
- Drehe die Karte um, lies das englische Wort und sage es.
- Du kannst das Wort in der App noch mal hören.

city	die Stadt, die Großstadt
town	die Stadt
street	die Straße
walk	(zu Fuß) gehen, wandern
bus	der Bus
underground	die U-Bahn
train	der Zug
car	das Auto
ticket	die Eintrittskarte, die Fahrkarte, das Ticket
free	kostenlos; frei
lots of	viel, viele
get around	herumkommen
see sights	Sehenswürdigkeiten sehen
visit a museum	ein Museum besuchen
buy a souvenir	ein Souvenir kaufen
walk across a bridge	über eine Brücke gehen

Berlin is a **city**.
Eisenach is a **town**.

London has **lots of sights**: the Tower Bridge, Big Ben, the British Museum, the London Eye, ...

So sagst du, wie du zur Schule, zum Jugendzentrum, ... kommst:

How do **you** get to school?	Wie kommst **du** zur Schule?
I get there by bus.	Ich fahre mit dem Bus (dorthin).
I walk there.	Ich gehe zu Fuß (dorthin).

So sagst du, was man in einer Stadt unternehmen kann:

What can **you** do in London?	Was kann **man** in London unternehmen?
What can **you** see or do there?	Was kann **man** dort sehen oder machen?
You can visit the British Museum.	**Man** kann das Britische Museum besuchen.

! ***You*** kann **du** oder **man** bedeuten.

▶ AH S. 18

Task: Our top 3 sights in London

Step 1 Look and read.

▶ Hilfe

Tower Bridge

You can get there by **train** or **bus**.
You can **walk across the bridge**.
You can **buy nice souvenirs**.

tickets: £6.70 (5–15 years)

👍 9

St James's Park

You can get there by **bus** or **tube**.
You can **buy a cold drink**.
You can **chill in the park**.

The park is free!

👍 6

Step 2 Prepare and write your post.

1. Pick a London sight. Find information on **page 16** and in **video 2**.

2. Write a post on a digital board.

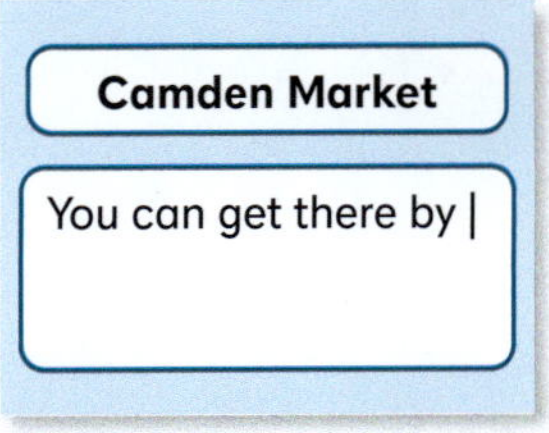

3. Find a photo of your London sight on the internet.

! Schreibe unter das Foto, wer es gemacht hat und woher es stammt (z. B. von einer Internetseite).
Beispiel:
Foto: Tina Muster,
http://London.example.com

Step 3 Read the posts. Vote for your 3 favourite sights.

👍 10

Jobs

1 Look and say.

I can see **lots of students**.
There is **a boy with red hair**.
There are **two blue chairs**.

→
- posters
- two white desks
- computers
- a green jacket
- ?

2 Read. Listen and answer.

▶ Audio 18

- What are Omar's favourite subjects?
- What are his hobbies?
- Who meets in room 52?

3 Listen and repeat.

▶ Audio 19

friendly

caring

hard-working

communicative

creative

reliable

good at working in a team

good at working alone

▶ Quiz

4 Play a game: What's missing?

▶ AH Bildkarten

5 a) Look and listen. Who is it?

▶ Audio 20

Tina

John

Emma

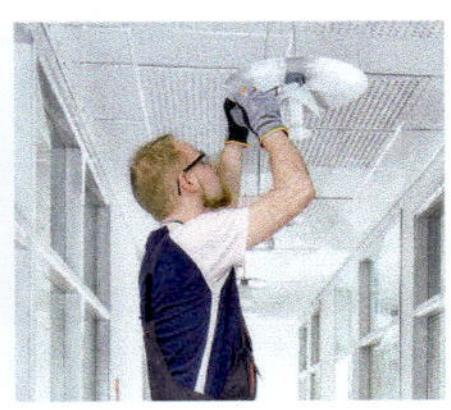
Connor

b) Listen again and say.

John is ______.

→ communicative • hard-working • reliable • good at working in a team

▶ AH S. 19

Jobs

1 **a) Listen to Omar and his friends.**

▶ Audio 21

b) Now you: Ask and answer.

What are your strong points?
- I'm ______.
- I'm very ______.

→ friendly • communicative • caring • hard-working • reliable • helpful • ?

I'm ...

☑ creative 🙂

☑ very creative 🙂🙂

▶ Quiz
▶ AH S. 20

2 **a) Listen to Mr Winter, Omar and his friends.**

▶ Audio 22

b) Now you: Ask and answer.

What are your strong points?
- I'm good at ______.
- I'm very good at ______.

→ working in a team • working alone • organizing • drawing • cooking • English • maths • science • art • ?

▶ Hilfe

▶ Quiz
▶ AH S. 21

3 Look. Listen to the song. Who is it?

▶ Audio 23–24

4 a) Listen to the students.

▶ Audio 25

b) Now you: Pick ideas. Talk to different partners.

You are (very) ______.

friendly • caring • reliable • creative • communicative • hard-working • cool • funny • clever • great • nice • helpful • honest • ?

You are (very) good at ______.

working in a team • working alone • cooking • cycling • chilling • swimming • football • science • German • ?

▶ AH S. 22

Jobs

1 Listen and repeat.

▶ Audio 26

restaurant

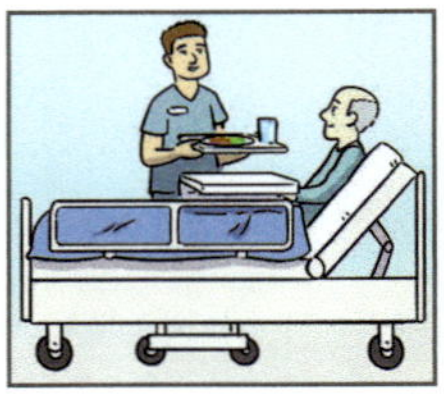

hospital

supermarket

garden centre

▶ Quiz
▶ AH S. 23

2 **a)** Listen to Omar and his sister.

▶ Audio 27

b) Now you: Ask and answer.

Where would you like to work?
– I'd like to work at ______.

Why would you like to work there?
– Because I'm (very) ______.

Where?	Why?
• a hospital • a supermarket • a cinema • an art shop • ?	• friendly • helpful • hard-working • good at maths • ?

▶ Hilfe

▶ Quiz
▶ AH S. 24

c) Write 2 sentences from **b)** in your exercise book.

3 Walk around. Talk about your neighbours, friends or family.

– My **neighbour** works at **a garden centre**.
– My **cousin** works at **a takeaway**.
– **Ryan** works at **a cinema**.

4 Look at the website. Answer in German.

Worum geht es auf der Website?

www.hey-trafford-school.example.net/jobs-for-students

▶ Hilfe

Can you walk my dog?

Every Monday!
£5 per day
Ms Wang

Your job:
Help in the garden!

Every Saturday
10–1 o'clock
Mr Walker

Your job:
Go shopping for my grandmother every Friday!

£5 per hour

Ron Martin

5 a) Read Omar's message and find ...

- die Begrüßung am Anfang
- die Person, die die Nachricht erhält
- den Gruß am Ende
- die Person, die die Nachricht schreibt.

Einen Brief oder eine E-Mail schreiben
- Begrüße die Person: *Dear Mr / Ms ...*
- Sage, worum es geht: *I would like ...*
- Schreibe einen Gruß und deinen Namen: *Best wishes ...*

▶ Hilfe

Dear Ms Wang,

I would like to have the job.
I'm 14 years old and I'm a student at Trafford School.
I like dogs and walking. I'm very friendly and reliable.
I can walk your dog every Monday at 4 o'clock.
My phone number is 07700 900638.

Best wishes
Omar

b) Read Omar's message again and say.

1 He likes ______ and ______.
2 He is very ______ and ______.

▶ AH S. 25

Football in Manchester

1 Look, read and say.

1 Omar ______ in Manchester.
2 He is a ______ ______ fan.
3 He watches ______ ______.

Manchester City

Manchester United

2 Listen to the podcast. It's about a football player.

▶ Audio 28

1 Who is Marcus Rashford?
2 What are his strong points?
3 Find photos of Marcus Rashford on the internet.

3 Life in Britain

In Großbritannien gibt es sehr viele Fußballfans.
Das größte Fußballmuseum der Welt ist in Manchester.
In **Manchester** gibt es zwei große und berühmte **Fußballvereine**: Manchester United und Manchester City. Die beiden Vereine sind fast 150 Jahre alt. Beide Vereine haben ein eigenes Stadion.
Beide Vereine haben Männer-Teams und Frauen-Teams.

- Welche Fußballspieler oder Fußballspielerinnen aus Großbritannien kennst du?
- Suche im Internet die Songs von Manchester United und Manchester City.

▶ AH S. 26

4 a) Cartoon: Listen and read along.

▶ Audio 29

- Why does Omar's grandmother like her job?
- What are Omar's strong points?

b) Act out the cartoon.

A good team

- Ich höre die Geschichte mehrmals. Ich spreche leise mit.
- Ich übe so lange, bis ich meine Rolle sicher sprechen kann.
- Ich übe zusammen mit anderen Schülern und Schülerinnen.
- Wir spielen die Geschichte und achten auf unsere Körpersprache.

▶ Sprech-Profi 1–2 S. 67
▶ AH S. 27

New words and phrases

Read and say.

▶ Hilfe

Wörter richtig schreiben
- Sieh dir das englische Wort genau an und schreibe es sorgfältig ab.
- Überprüfe das Wort, Buchstabe für Buchstabe.
- Viele englische Wörter schreibt man anders, als man sie spricht.
- Schreibe diese Wörter mehrmals und markiere die schwierigen Stellen: *friendly, reliable, ...*

friendly	freundlich
communicative	kommunikativ, aufgeschlossen
creative	kreativ
hard-working	arbeitsam, fleißig
reliable	zuverlässig
good at working in a team	gut darin, im Team zu arbeiten
good at working alone	gut darin, allein zu arbeiten
caring	fürsorglich, liebevoll, warmherzig
restaurant	das Restaurant
hospital	das Krankenhaus
supermarket	der Supermarkt
garden centre	das Gartencenter; die Gärtnerei
job	der Job, die (Arbeits-)Stelle
Dear ...	Lieber / Liebe ...
Best wishes	Viele Grüße

Achte beim Sprechen darauf, wo die Betonung eines Wortes liegt. Das ist wichtig bei Wörtern mit 2 oder mehr Silben:
cre·a·tive
re·li·a·ble
com·mu·ni·ca·tive

So sagst du, was deine Stärken sind:

What are your strong points?	Was sind deine Stärken?
I'm creative.	Ich bin kreativ.
I'm very reliable.	Ich bin sehr zuverlässig.

So sagst du, wo du gerne arbeiten würdest und warum:

Where would you like to work?	Wo würdest du gerne arbeiten?
I'd like to work at a hospital.	Ich würde gerne in einem Krankenhaus arbeiten.
Why would you like to work there?	Warum würdest du gerne dort arbeiten?
Because I'm caring and reliable.	Weil ich fürsorglich und zuverlässig bin.

▶ AH S. 28

Task: Talk about jobs

Step 1 Watch the video.

▶ Video 3

Hello, I'm **Ms Green**.
What's your name? How old are you?
– Hello, **Ms Green**. I'm **Ben** and I'm **14**.
OK, **Ben**. What are your strong points?
– I'm very **communicative**.
Great. Where would you like to work?
– I'd like to work at **a supermarket**.
Why would you like to work there?
– Because I'm good at **maths**.
What about a job at **a shopping centre**?
– That's a good idea. Thank you.

Step 2 Practise with a partner. Use a dialogue card.

▶ AH Dialogkarte

Step 3 Act out your dialogue. Give and take feedback.

Du kannst dein **Feedback** auf Englisch oder auf Deutsch geben.
Auf Seite 82 findest du mehr Ideen für dein Feedback.

▶ Classroom English S. 82

Free time

1 Look and say.

I can see **a bridge**.
There is **a bike**.
There are **three cars**.

→ a blue and yellow bus • an orange rucksack • white socks • yellow shorts • a green skirt • ?

2 Read. Listen and answer.

▶ Audio 30

- What sports does Grace like?
- What sports does Tom like?
- And you? What sports do you like?

3 Listen and repeat.

▶ Audio 31

week – weekend

play cards

watch a series

chill at home

do karate

do my nails

have dinner with my family

go hiking

▶ Quiz
▶ AH S. 29

4 Play a game: Mime it!

▶ AH Bildkarten

5 Listen. Talk to a partner.

▶ Audio 32

▶ AH S. 30

Free time

1 a) Listen to Grace and her friends.

▶ Audio 33

b) Now you: Ask and answer.

Did you ______
last weekend?
– Yes, I did.
– No, I didn't.

→ chill at home • do karate • do your nails • go hiking • have dinner with your family • play cards • watch a series

▶ Quiz

2 Now you: Ask and answer in class.

→

Did you	go swimming • go shopping • ...	last week?
	play computer games • play football • ...	
	do your hair • do sport • ...	
	have dinner with your family / neighbours	
	meet friends • eat pizza • ...	

▶ AH S. 31

3 a) Learning English

Verhaltensregeln auf Englisch verstehen

- Welche Wörter verstehst du?
- Sieh dir die Bilder an. Sie helfen dir beim Verstehen.
- Symbole haben in vielen Ländern die gleiche Bedeutung.
- Finde diese Symbole auf den Schildern und Plakaten unten:

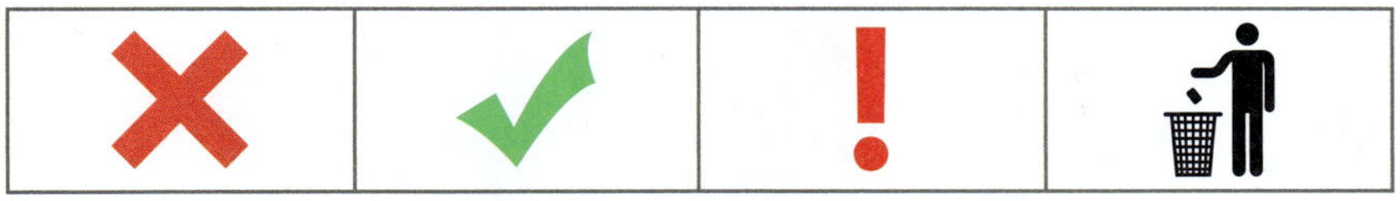

b) Look at the signs in a). Answer in German.

1. *Wann findet die Aktion in Inverness statt?*
2. *Was soll man mit seinem Müll machen?*
3. *Wer kann bei den Aktionen mithelfen?*

4 Listen to Grace and Tom. Answer.

1. Did Grace do her beach clean-up?
2. Did she find a plastic chair?
3. Did she find an old shoe?

▶ Audio 34

▶ AH S. 32

Free time

1 a) Listen to Grace and her friends.

▶ Audio 35

b) Now you: Ask and answer.

What did you do last week?

– I ______.

→

• play**ed** cards	• **did** karate
• watch**ed** a series	• **did** my nails
• chill**ed** at home	• **had** dinner
	• **went** hiking

▶ Hilfe
▶ Quiz
▶ AH S. 33

2 Now you: Ask and answer in class.

I	clean**ed** my bike • walk**ed** my dog • ...	last week. / last weekend.
	play**ed** table tennis • play**ed** basketball • ...	
	did my hair • **did** sport • ...	
	had dinner with my family / friends / ...	
	went shopping • **went** swimming • ...	

▶ AH S. 34

3 Listen and repeat.

▶ Audio 36

turn left | go straight on | turn right

4 a) Listen and look at the map. Find the places.

▶ Audio 37

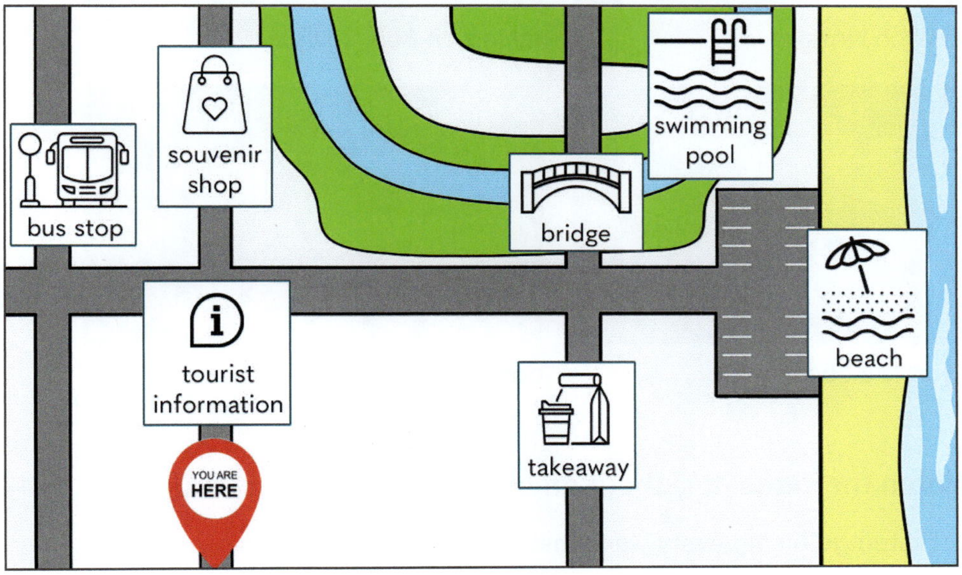

b) Listen to Grace and a tourist.

▶ Audio 38

Excuse me. How do I get to the **bus stop**?

Go straight on, turn **left**, and then turn **right**.

Thank you.

You're welcome.

c) Now you: Talk to a partner about the places in a).

Excuse me. How do I get to the ________?
– Go straight on, turn **right**, and then turn **left**.
Thank you.
– You're welcome.

→
- beach
- bridge
- souvenir shop
- swimming pool
- takeaway

▶ Quiz
▶ AH S. 35

Outdoor activities in Scotland

1 **Look and find …**

- the rucksacks
- the skirts
- the red jackets
- the bike

visiting Loch Ness

hiking on Ben Nevis

cycling at the coast

dancing at the Highland Games

2 **Watch the video. It's about an outdoor centre in Scotland.** ▶ Video 4

1 Did Kirsten go hiking every week last summer?
2 When did Kirsten go camping?
3 Did Ron go swimming in Loch Ness last summer?

3 **Life in Britain**

Schottland hat eine vielfältige Landschaft. An der Küste gibt es Strände, hohe Klippen und viele Inseln. Im Landesinneren gibt es hohe Berge. Dazwischen liegen große Seen. Der berühmteste See heißt *Loch Ness*. Der höchste Berg heißt *Ben Nevis*.
Im Norden von Schottland finden jedes Jahr die *Highland Games* statt. Das sind sportliche Wettkämpfe mit Musik und Tanz.
Bei den *Highland Games* gibt es besondere Sportarten wie Baumstammwerfen, Tauziehen und Fassrollen.

- Welche Berge oder Seen kennst du?
- Welche Outdoor-Aktivität möchtest du ausprobieren?

▶ AH S. 36

4 Cartoon: Listen and read along.

▶ Audio 39

1 What did the class do?
2 Did Grace and her friends have a map?
3 When were Grace and her friends at the museum?

Tipp
they were =
sie waren

An exciting hiking tour

Last summer, Grace and her class went on a tour to Loch Ness.
First they **went hiking**. Then they **had a picnic** next to the water.

At 2.30, all students **were at the museum**. They were happy and tired!

- Ich sehe mir die Bilder an und lese die Überschrift. Worum geht es?
- Ich lese die Fragen. Was soll ich herausfinden?
- Ich lese den Text genau. Ich achte auf die **Schlüsselwörter**.

▶ Lese-Profi 1–2 S. 68
▶ AH S. 37

New words and phrases

Read and say.

► Hilfe
► AH Bildkarten

Wörter mit einem Laufdiktat üben

1. Hänge 4 Wort-Karten auf.
   Sieh dir eine Wort-Karte an: Lies das Wort.
2. Merke dir das Wort und gehe zu deinem Tisch.
3. Schreibe das Wort auf.
4. Überprüfe mithilfe der Wörterliste:
   Hast du das Wort richtig geschrieben?

week	die Woche
weekend	das Wochenende
play cards	Karten spielen
watch a series	eine Serie schauen
chill at home	zu Hause chillen
do karate	Karate machen
do my nails	meine (Finger-)Nägel machen
have dinner with my family	mit meiner Familie Abend essen
go hiking	wandern gehen
Excuse me, ...	Entschuldigung, ...
go straight on	geradeaus gehen (fahren)
turn left / right	nach links / rechts abbiegen
then	dann

I do **my** nails.
You do **your** nails.
She does **her** nails.
He does **his** nails.
...

So fragst du, ob jemand etwas gemacht hat:

Did you watch a series last weekend?	Hast du letztes Wochenende eine Serie geschaut?
Yes, I **did**.	Ja.
No, I **didn't**.	Nein.

! Die Frage *Did you ...?* beantwortest du höflich mit *Yes, I did.* oder *No, I didn't.*

So sagst du, was du gemacht hast:

What **did** you do last week?	Was hast du letzte Woche gemacht?
I play**ed** cards. I chill**ed** at home.	Ich habe Karten gespielt. Ich habe zu Hause gechillt.
I **did** karate. I **had** lunch. I **went** hiking.	Ich habe Karate gemacht. Ich habe Mittag gegessen. Ich bin wandern gegangen.

! Die meisten Verben haben in der Vergangenheit ein **-ed** am Ende. Manche Verben haben besondere Formen: *did, had, went*.

► AH S. 38

Task: My 3 highlights last week

Step 1 Listen and read along.

▶ Audio 40

Last **Wednesday** I **did karate**.
Last **Friday** I **played cards with my brother**.
On **Saturday** I **went hiking with my friend Liz**.
I had a **great** week!

Step 2 Make notes about your activities last week.

1. What did you do last week?

MON: played football with Ben
TUE: watched a series
WED: did my homework
THU: went shopping
FRI: cleaned my room
SAT: chilled at home
SUN: had dinner with my family

2. Mark your 3 favourite activities.

MON: played football with Ben ☺
TUE: watched a series
WED: did my homework
THU: went shopping ☺
FRI: cleaned my room
SAT: chilled at home
SUN: had dinner with my family ☺

Benutze eine **Wörterbuch-App**, wenn du ein Wort nicht weiβt.

Step 3 Record your voice note.

Benutze eine **Aufnahme-App**:
- Sprich deutlich.
- Mache kurze Pausen zwischen den Sätzen.
- Höre deine Aufnahme an: Sprichst du deutlich? Machst du Pausen?

Step 4 Play your voice note. Give and take feedback.

▶ Classroom English S. 82

Digital life

1 Look and say.

I can see **Dylan's room**.
There is **a yellow sofa**.
There are **lots of clothes**.

→ a grey desk • a blue door • a lamp • an orange chair • an apple • books • cushions • green socks • shelves • ?

2 Read. Listen and answer.

▶ Audio 41

- Who has 96 points?
- What day is it?
- Did Dylan walk the dog?

- And you: Do you like playing online games?
- What do you do with your friends?

3 Listen and repeat.

▶ Audio 42

chat with friends	follow people	talk to my mum	buy things online	post comments

look for information	check the time	take photos	make videos	write emails

▶ Quiz
▶ AH S. 39

4 Listen. Talk to a partner.

▶ Audio 43

What do you do on your phone?

I **chat with friends** and **follow people**.
I **take photos** too.

5 Listen and read. Who is it?

▶ Audio 44

– It's **Amira**. **She chats with friends**, **follows people** and ...

	Amira	Ella	Luca	Rico
chats with friends	✓	✓	✓	
follows people	✓	✓		✓
posts comments		✓	✓	✓
buys things online				✓
takes photos	✓		✓	

▶ AH S. 40

Digital life

1 a) Listen to Dylan and his friends.

▶ Audio 45

b) Now you: Mime it. Ask and answer in class.

→

I'm	chat**ting** with friends.
	tak**ing** photos.
	buy**ing** things online.
	listen**ing** to music.
	talk**ing** to my mum / dad.
	play**ing** online games. • play**ing** football.
	do**ing** karate. • do**ing** my nails.
	drink**ing** tea. • ?

▶ Quiz
▶ AH S. 41

2 Look and listen.

▶ Audio 46

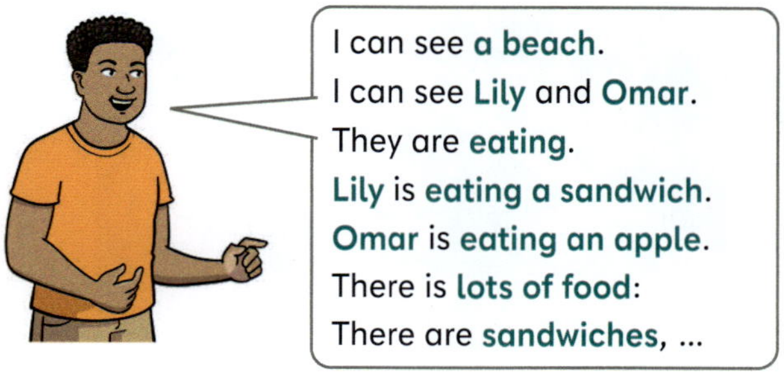

3 Learning English

Ein Bild beschreiben

- Sieh dir das Bild in Ruhe an.
- Beschreibe, welche Orte, Personen und Dinge du siehst:
  I can see a beach. / There is a chair. / There are lots of people.
- Beschreibe, was die Personen auf dem Bild gerade machen:
  *She **is** eating a sandwich. He **is** taking a photo. They **are** eating.*
- Probiere es mit den Bildern in Aufgabe 4 aus.

4 Look and say. What can you see? What are the people doing?

▶ Hilfe

Dylan • teacher • Owen

Dylan • shop assistant

▶ AH S. 42–43

Digital life

1 Listen to Dylan and his mother. Answer.

1 What is Dylan's mother doing?
2 What is Dylan doing?
3 What's for dinner?

▶ Audio 47

2 Learning English

Mit Familie und Freunden telefonieren

- Das sagst du zur Begrüßung:
  Hi, … . Hello, … . It's me, Dylan.
- Frage nach, wenn du etwas nicht verstehst:
  Sorry, I can't hear you. Can you say that again, please?
- Verabschiede dich:
  Bye. / See you (later).
- Welche von diesen Sätzen hörst du in den Gesprächen in den Aufgaben 1 und 3?

3 a) Listen and read along.

▶ Audio 48

Owen: Hi, Dylan. It's me, Owen.
Dylan: Hi, Owen. What are you doing?
Owen: I'm making a video for history on Friday.
Dylan: Sorry, I can't hear you. Can you say that again, please?
Owen: I'm making a history video for school. I'm in town. Can you help me?
Dylan: Yes, I can help you.
Owen: Thank you, Dylan. Let's meet at the art museum at 5 o'clock.
Dylan: OK. Bye! See you later.

b) Watch the video.
Now you: Make a dialogue with your partner.

▶ Video 5
▶ Quiz
▶ AH S. 44

4 Look at the pictures. Listen and find.

▶ Audio 49

What's the right picture?

- tap to open the app
- switch off the sound
- connect to Wi-Fi
- enter your password
- upload a photo
- delete a post

5 Learning English

Englisch als Internetsprache
Im Internet werden sehr viele englische Wörter verwendet. Das liegt daran, dass Englisch eine **Weltsprache** ist: Viele Menschen auf der Welt sprechen oder verstehen Englisch, auch wenn Englisch nicht ihre Erstsprache ist. Menschen aus verschiedenen Ländern verständigen sich deshalb im Internet auf Englisch.
Sieh dir die folgenden Begriffe an:

online website follower likes social media
chat log out user like
link hacker fake photos
upload app download
account offline
log in hotspot fake news

- Welche Begriffe kennst du?
- Was bedeuten sie?
- Fallen dir noch andere Begriffe ein?

▶ AH S. 45

Things to do and see in Wales

1 Look and find ...

- the water
- the train
- the rugby ball
- the bridge

There are great national parks.

You can visit old castles.

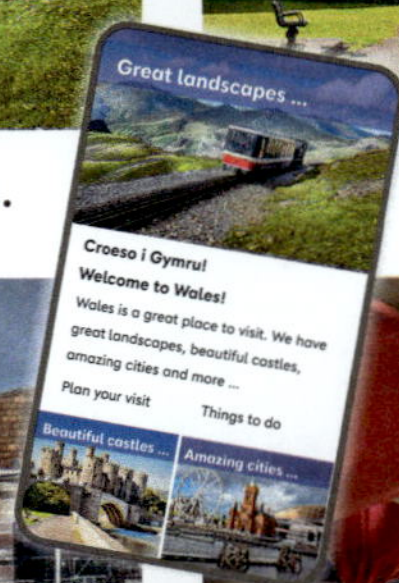

Cardiff is the capital of Wales.

You can watch a rugby game.

2 Watch the video. It's about rugby.

► Video 6

- When did Dylan watch the rugby game in Cardiff?
- Does Dylan like playing rugby online?

3 Life in Britain

Wales ist ein beliebtes Reiseziel. Dort gibt es viele Nationalparks. In Wales leben mehr Schafe als Menschen! Es gibt auch viele alte Burgen und Schlösser. Viele Touristen benutzen eine Reise-App, wenn sie sich über Wales informieren wollen.

Die Hauptstadt *(capital)* von Wales ist Cardiff. Cardiff ist die größte Stadt in Wales. Im *Principality Stadium* in Cardiff finden wichtige Rugby-Spiele statt. Rugby ist in Wales sehr beliebt.

- Hast du schon einmal ein Rugby-Spiel gesehen?
- Suche im Internet Informationen über Wales:
  Wie viele Einwohner hat Cardiff?
  Welche Sprachen stehen auf den Schildern in Wales?

► AH S. 46

4 Cartoon: Listen and read along.

▶ Audio 50

1 What are Dylan and Owen doing at the car show?
2 Does Dylan's family have a new car?
3 Does Owen like Dylan's first photo on social media?

Tipp
like =
1. mögen,
2. liken
3. der Like

Dylan's cool photo

It's Sunday. Owen and Dylan are at the Llandudno Car Show. They are taking lots of photos.

Owen sends Dylan the photo.

It's Tuesday. Owen and a friend are looking at Dylan's social media account.

Later Dylan deletes the fake photo and posts Owen's photo.
The next day, Dylan checks his social media account: 50 people liked the photo. That's OK for Dylan too.

▶ AH S. 47

New words and phrases

Read and say.

▶ Hilfe

Wörter im Zusammenhang lernen

- Du kannst einzelne Wörter lernen, wie z. B. *post* = posten.
- Besser lernst du Wörter, wenn du sie mit anderen Wörtern verbindest: *post a comment* = einen Kommentar posten
- Verbinde das neue Wort auch mit anderen Wörtern: *post a photo, post a video, …*

▶ Quiz

chat with friends	mit Freunden chatten; sich mit Freunden unterhalten
follow people	Leuten (online) folgen
buy things online	Dinge online kaufen
post a comment	einen Kommentar posten
look for information	Informationen suchen
talk to my mum	mit meiner Mutter sprechen
check the time	die Uhrzeit nachschauen
write an email	eine E-Mail schreiben
take a photo	ein Foto machen
make a video	ein Video machen

Manchmal schreibt man das **-t** doppelt: *cha**t**: cha**tt**ing, cha**tt**ed*

information = die Information, die Informationen

E: ***take*** *a photo*
D: ein Foto **machen**

So sagst du, was du gerade machst:

What **are** you do**ing**?	Was machst du (gerade)?
I'm taking photos.	Ich mache (gerade) Fotos.

So sagst du, was andere gerade machen:

He (Dylan) **is** She (Lily) **is** They **are**	chill**ing**.	Er chillt (gerade). Sie chillt (gerade). Sie chillen (gerade).

! Bei der Verlaufsform hängst du **-ing** an das Verb. Das **-e** am Ende entfällt: take – tak**ing**, write – writ**ing**, …

So telefonierst du mit Familie und Freunden:

It's me.	Ich bin's.
Sorry, I can't hear you.	Tut mir leid. Ich kann dich nicht hören.
Can you say that again, please?	Kannst du das bitte noch mal sagen?
See you. / See you later.	Bis dann. / Bis später.

▶ AH S. 48

Task: Chatting with a friend

Step 1 Look and read.

▶ Hilfe

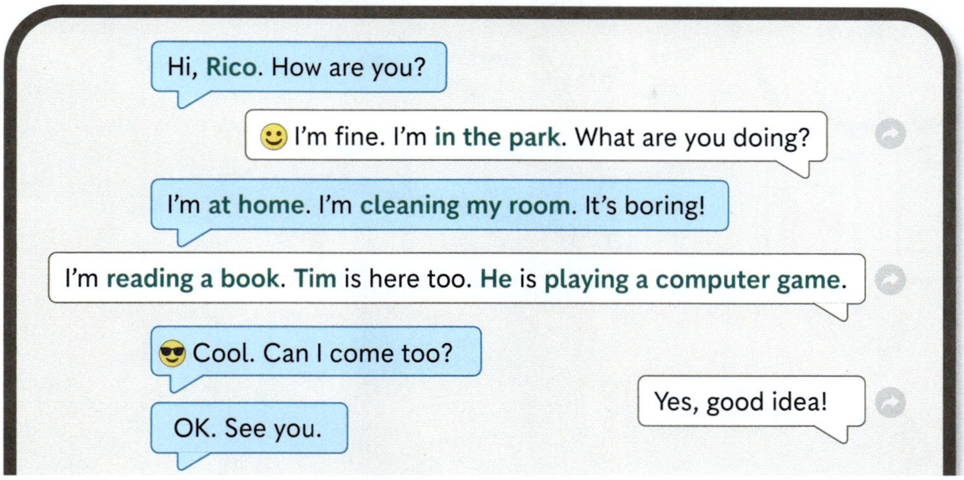

▶ Schreib-Profi 1 S. 69

Step 2 Write a chat with your partner. Pick ideas.

I'm ...	I'm ...
• in the park • at home • at the youth centre • at the skate park	• buying things online • doing my homework • watching a show • making dinner

Ihr könnt euren **Chat** direkt in eine App schreiben oder auf Papier notieren.

▶ Schreib-Profi 2 S. 69

Step 3 Check your chat messages.

- Ich überprüfe meine Sätze. Habe ich alles richtig geschrieben?
- Kann ich alles verstehen?
- In einem Chat kann ich meine Beiträge leicht verbessern oder löschen.

▶ Schreib-Profi 3 S. 69

Step 4 Present your chat to the class. Give and take feedback.

▶ Classroom English S. 82

Friends

1 Look and say.

What can you see?
- I can see **six people**. → a train • a table • books • numbers • two phones • posters • ?
- There is **a shop**. There are **books**.

What are Lily and Orla doing?
- **Lily** is **taking a photo**. → taking a photo • checking the time • looking for information • ?
- Lily and Orla are **talking**.

2 Read. Listen and answer.

▶ Audio 51

- Where is Lily?
- Why does Orla like her town?
- How do Lily and Orla get to Orla's home?

- And you? Do you like your town or city? ☆ Why (not)?
- Do all your friends live in your town or city?

3 Listen and repeat.

▶ Audio 52

call you every day

answer your messages

say nice things about you

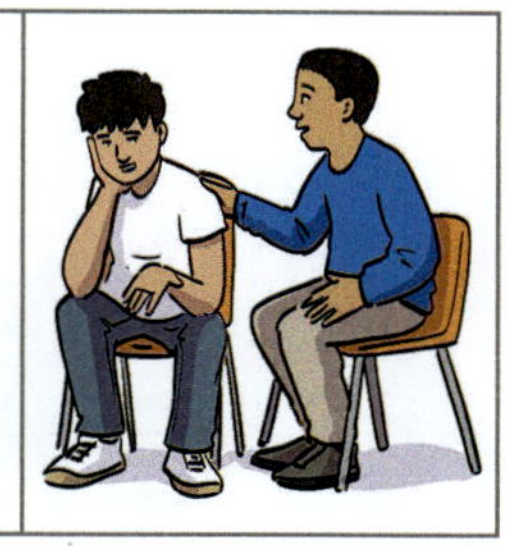

talk about problems

understand you

give you presents

lend you things

wear cool clothes

▶ Quiz

4 Walk around. Ask and answer with different partners.

▶ AH Bildkarten

▶ AH S. 49

Friends

1 a) **Listen to Lily and her friends.**

▶ Audio 53

b) **Now you: Talk to a partner.**

A good friend should ______. →

- I agree.
  That's very important.
- I **don't** agree.
  That's **not** important.

- understand you
- say nice things
- talk about problems
- give you presents
- answer your messages
- lend you things
- wear cool clothes
- call you every day

▶ Quiz
▶ AH S. 50

2 a) **Read Lily's text about good friends.
Do you agree?**

b) **What's important for you? Write in your exercise book.**

A good friend should
talk about problems.

A good friend should
answer your messages.

A good friend should
help you.

→

- help you
- listen to you
- do sports with you
- look after your cat
- go to the cinema with you
- play games with you
- make dinner for you
- ?

▶ AH S. 51

3 a) Look and read. Find the 3 phrases in the song.

Was könnten die 3 Phrasen bedeuten?

That's what friends are for

1 (...) Keep smiling, keep shining
2 Knowing you can always count on me, for sure
3 That's what friends are for
4 For good times and bad times
5 I'll be on your side forever more
6 That's what friends are for (...)

(from a song by Burt Bacharach and Carol Bayer Sager)

Tipp
that's what friends are for = dafür sind Freunde da

b) Find the song on the internet. Listen and answer.

1 What are friends for?
- for good times
- for bad times
- for good and bad times

2 Do you like the song?

Schreibe „*That's what friends are for*" und „1985" in die Suchmaschine.
Tipp: Der Textausschnitt von **3a** beginnt im Song nach ca. 1 Minute.

4 Learning English

Eine Wörterbuch-App benutzen

- Wenn du englische Songs hörst, musst du nicht jedes Wort kennen.
- Du kannst Wörter in einer Wörterbuch-App nachsehen.
- Stelle die passende Suchrichtung ein: Englisch – Deutsch.
- Manchmal hat ein Wort mehrere Bedeutungen.
- Welche Bedeutung passt gut?
- Suche diese Phrasen: *count on, for sure, bad times.*

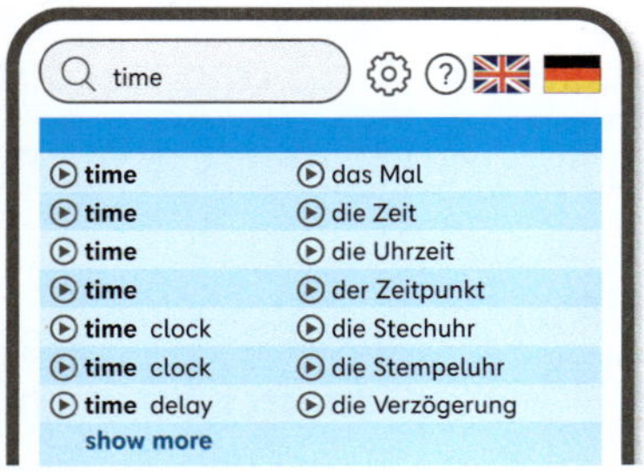

▶ AH S. 52

Friends

1 Listen and repeat. ▶ Audio 54

relaxed | amazing | positive | active

▶ Quiz

2 **a)** Listen to Orla and her friend. ▶ Audio 55

b) Now you: Talk to a partner.

I like Mo because he is ______.
I like Olivia because she is ______.

→ relaxed • amazing • positive • active • friendly • caring • honest • ?

▶ AH S. 53

3 **a)** Listen to Orla and her father. ▶ Audio 56

Orla likes / doesn't like ______ because it's ______.

→

Orla Orla's father	likes **doesn't** like	gaming history	because it's	exciting. boring. important.

▶ AH S. 54

b) What do or don't you like? Tell your class. ▶ Hilfe

I like / don't like ______ because it's ______.

4 Look and read.

- What is SportBoy's problem?
- Does Alison understand SportBoy's problem?

▶ Hilfe

Talk about problems | Ask Alison

Dear Alison,
My best friend is cool and relaxed. Last summer we did lots of sport together. But this summer he plays computer games every day.
We don't meet for sport and he doesn't answer my messages.
What should I do?
Best wishes
SportBoy

Dear SportBoy,
I understand your problem.
I think you should talk to your friend or write a message: "Let's meet for sport one day a week."
Your friend doesn't answer?
Talk to a social worker at school.
Best wishes
Alison

5 a) Watch the video.

▶ Video 7

Die eigene Meinung sagen

- Trau dich, in einer Diskussion deine Meinung zu sagen.
- Sei dabei immer höflich.
- Auf Englisch kannst du sagen: *I agree. / Sorry, I don't agree. I think … / I don't think …*

▶ Classroom English S. 82

b) Do you agree with Alison? Talk in groups.

- I agree.
- Sorry, I don't agree.

→ I think SportBoy should	talk to his friend.
	talk to a social worker.
	call his friend every day.
I don't think SportBoy should	play computer games with his friend.
	?

▶ Hilfe

▶ AH S. 55

Visiting Ireland

1 Look and find ...

- the green hair
- the brown horse
- the red doors
- the white trousers

St Patrick's Day in Dublin

King John's Castle in Limerick

horses near the River Shannon

Irish folk music

2 Watch the video. It's about things to do and see in Limerick.

▶ Video 8

1 Does the castle close on Mondays?
2 Does Orla like graffiti?
3 What are your favourite things to do or see in your town or city?

3 Life in Britain

Die **Republik Irland** ist ein Staat auf der Insel Irland.
Am 17. März feiert man in Irland den *Saint Patrick's Day*. An diesem Tag ist alles grün dekoriert. Häufig sieht man das dreiblättrige Kleeblatt. Das ist ein Symbol für Irland.
Die traditionelle irische Musik nennt man *Irish folk music*. Die typischen Instrumente sind Geige, Trommel und Flöte.

- Finde die Stadt **Limerick** und den Fluss **Shannon** auf der **Landkarte** hinten im Buch.
- Suche *„Irish folk music"* im Internet und höre dir die Musik an. Gefällt dir die Musik?

▶ Karte: United Kingdom, Ireland

▶ AH S. 56

4 a) **Story: Listen and read along.**

What's the radio show about?

▶ Audio 57

b) **Act out the story's dialogue with a partner. You can use dialogue cards.**

▶ AH Dialogkarten

The radio show

Lily and Orla are listening to Orla's favourite radio show, the Morning Show. This week the show is about good friends. You can call in and talk about your friends. Every day, you can win tickets for a big party.

Tessa: This is the Morning Show on Radio Blue. I'm Tessa. Who is calling?

Lily: Hello. I'm Lily. My friend's name is Orla. We would like to go to the party.

Tessa: Great. Tell me about your friend. Why do you like Orla?

Lily: Because she is very active. She is relaxed too.

Tessa: Does she call you every day?

Lily: Yes, she does. She talks about problems and she understands me.

Tessa: I think that's very important. Your friend Orla has lots of strong points. She is amazing! You and Orla can go to our big party.

Lily: Great! Thank you, Tessa.

Orla and Lily are very happy. And they are excited about the party!

- Wir hören die Geschichte mehrmals an. Wir sprechen leise mit.
- Wir ersetzen die **türkisblauen Wörter** durch unsere eigenen Ideen.
- Wir üben, bis wir unsere Rollen sicher sprechen können.

▶ Sprech-Profi 1–2 S. 67
▶ AH S. 57

New words and phrases

Read and say.

▶ Hilfe

Wörter mit einer Mindmap wiederholen

- Schreibe das Thema in die Mitte, z. B. *friends*.
- Schreibe die Oberbegriffe auf die Seitenarme, z. B. *strong points, what we do, …*
- Du weißt einen Oberbegriff nicht? Schaue ihn nach oder male ein Bild.
- Schreibe die Wörter und Phrasen zu den Oberbegriffen.

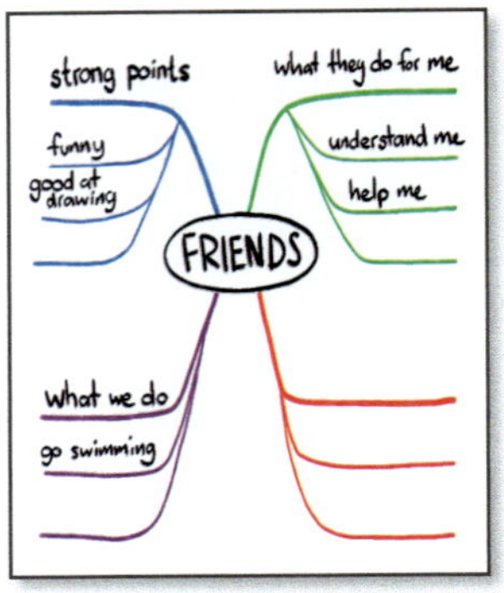

▶ Quiz

call you (every day)	dich (jeden Tag) anrufen
answer your messages	auf deine Nachrichten antworten
say nice things about you	nette Dinge über dich sagen
talk about problems	über Probleme sprechen
understand you	dich verstehen
give you presents	dir Geschenke geben
lend you things	dir Dinge leihen
wear cool clothes	coole Kleidung tragen
relaxed	entspannt, locker
amazing	großartig, toll, erstaunlich
positive	positiv
active	aktiv
best friend	bester Freund, beste Freundin
I think …	Ich denke / finde, …

So sagst du, was jemand tun sollte:

A good friend **should** understand you.	Ein guter Freund / Eine gute Freundin **sollte** dich verstehen.

Und so stimmst du zu oder nicht:

I agree. That's very important.	Ich stimme (dir) zu. Das ist sehr wichtig.
I don't agree. That's not important.	Ich stimme (dir) nicht zu. Das ist nicht wichtig.

So sagst du, warum du jemanden magst:

I like Nina **because** she is very relaxed.	Ich mag Nina, **weil** sie sehr entspannt ist.

▶ AH S. 58

Task: A poster about friends

Step 1 Look and read.

▶ Hilfe

Step 2 Prepare and make your poster.

1. Collect ideas and make notes.
2. Draw or find pictures.
3. Make your poster.

Auf den Seiten 28 und 58 findest du passende Wörter.
Du kannst dein **Plakat** auf Papier oder in einer **App** gestalten.

Step 3 Present your poster. Give and take feedback.

▶ Classroom English S. 82

The weather

1 **Listen and repeat.** ▶ Audio 58

weather | It's hot. | It's warm. | It's cold. | It's 15 degrees.

It's sunny. | It's rainy. | It's windy. | It's cloudy. | It's snowy.

▶ Quiz
▶ AH S. 59 Nr. 1

2 **a) Look and listen.** ▶ Audio 59

b) Now you: Ask and answer. ▶ AH Bildkarten

What's the weather like?

- It's cold and rainy.
- It's 15 degrees.

c) Look out of the window. What's the weather like today?

▶ AH S. 59 Nr. 2

3 a) Watch the video. It's about the weather in Europe.

▶ Video 9

b) Watch the video again. Answer.

What's the weather like in **London**?
- It's **cold** and **windy** in **London**.
- It's **14** degrees.

→ Copenhagen • Warsaw • Berlin • Amsterdam • Paris

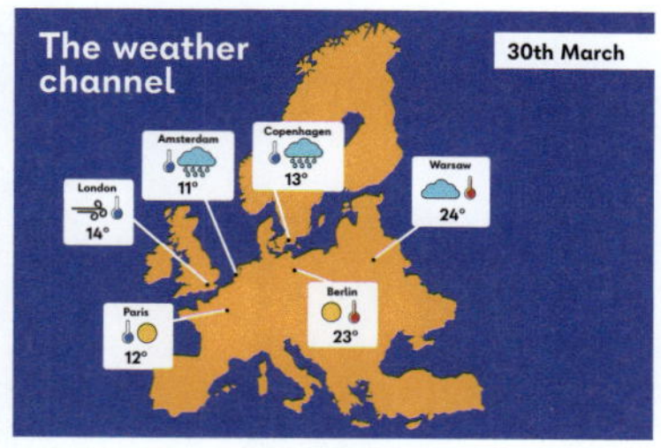

4 a) Look and listen.

▶ Audio 60

b) Look at the map in **a)**. Ask and answer.

Where is **Paris**?
- **Paris** is in **France**.
- **Paris** is the capital of **France**.

→ France • the Netherlands • Germany • Poland • Denmark • the United Kingdom (the UK)

Englisch und andere Sprachen

Viele **Ländernamen** sind im Englischen ähnlich wie in anderen Sprachen. Sieh dir die **Europa-Karte** auf Seite 86 an:
- Welche Ländernamen sind ähnlich wie im Deutschen?
- Welche Ländernamen kennst du in anderen Sprachen?

▶ Europa-Karte S. 86

▶ AH S. 60

c) Pick 3 capitals. Write sentences from **b)** in your exercise book.

Darts

1 a) Look. Listen to Dylan and Owen. Answer.

▶ Audio 61

1 Does Dylan like darts?
2 Who is Owen's favourite sport star? Fallon Sherrock or Olli Lawrence?
3 What about you? Do you like watching or playing darts?

b) Walk around. Ask and answer with different partners.

Who is your favourite sport star?
– My favourite sport star is ______.

2 a) Read the profile.

▶ Hilfe

name:	Fallon Sherrock
birthday:	2nd July
from:	England
sport:	darts
hobbies:	She likes listening (and dancing) to pop music.
strong points:	She is very positive and creative. She is friendly with her fans. She is funny.
fun fact:	Some people say she is "the queen of the palace".

b) Write a profile about your favourite sport star.

▶ AH S. 61

Earth Day

1 a) Look and listen.

▶ Audio 62

When is Earth Day?

b) Look at the slogans in a). Answer in German.

1 *Welche Art der Ernährung ist gut für die Erde?*
2 *Warum ist die Erde wichtig für uns?*
3 *Welche Verkehrsmittel sollten wir am meisten nutzen?*

c) Write and draw slogans for your classroom.

Benutze eine **Wörterbuch-App**. Dort kannst du unbekannte Wörter nachschauen und anhören.

2 Celebrations

Der **Earth Day** wird seit 1970 am 22. April gefeiert. An diesem Tag beschäftigen sich viele Menschen auf der ganzen Welt mit dem Thema Umweltschutz. Viele Menschen starten Aktionen: Sie sammeln Müll oder pflanzen Bäume. Manche bauen auch ein Insektenhotel oder einen Nistkasten für Vögel.

- Hast du schon einmal an solchen Aktionen teilgenommen?
- Was kannst du mit deiner Klasse für die Umwelt tun?

▶ AH S. 62

Halloween

1 a) Look and find ...

- the red hair
- the green glasses
- the braces
- the grey skirt

b) Look at a) and listen. Say.

▶ Audio 63

Lily is wearing **a green jacket**, **a green skirt** and **black shoes**.

☆ **She** has **long black hair**.

→ a skirt • a jacket • a cap • a sweatshirt • a T-shirt • shoes • socks • jeans • trousers

2 Celebrations

Halloween wird seit über 1000 Jahren gefeiert. Die Tradition kommt ursprünglich aus Irland. Irische Einwandernde brachten Halloween im 19. Jahrhundert in die USA. Inzwischen feiert man Halloween in vielen Ländern.

In der Stadt Derry in Nordirland feiert man jedes Jahr das größte Halloween-Festival in Europa. Es gibt viele Stände und Attraktionen und einen großen Halloween-Umzug. Dort sieht man viele gruselige oder lustige Verkleidungen.

- Suche im Internet nach Bildern vom Halloween-Festival in Derry.
- Welche Verkleidung gefällt dir besonders gut?

▶ AH S. 63

New words and phrases

Read and say.

▶ Hilfe

Englische Adjektive mit -y

- Mit der Endung **-y** kann man Adjektive aus Nomen bilden: *wind → windy, snow → snowy*
- Finde weitere Adjektive mit der Endung **-y** auf dieser Seite.
- Wie heißen die passenden englischen Nomen?
- Überprüfe deine Antworten mit einer Wörterbuch-App.

weather	das Wetter
warm	warm
sunny	sonnig
rainy	regnerisch
windy	windig
cloudy	bewölkt, wolkig
snowy	schneebedeckt, verschneit
Europe	Europa
capital	die Hauptstadt
France	Frankreich
the Netherlands	die Niederlande
Poland	Polen
Denmark	Dänemark
the United Kingdom (the UK)	das Vereinigte Königreich

▶ Europa-Karte S. 86

So sprichst du über das Wetter:

What's the weather like (today)?	Wie ist das Wetter (heute)?
What's the weather like in Berlin?	Wie ist das Wetter in Berlin?
It's cold and cloudy	Es ist kalt und bewölkt.
It's hot and sunny.	Es ist heiß und sonnig.
It's 1 degree. / **It's** 15 degrees.	**Es ist** 1 Grad. / **Es sind** 15 Grad.

So sprichst du über Länder und ihre Hauptstädte:

Paris is in France.	Paris ist in Frankreich.
Paris is the capital of France.	Paris ist die Hauptstadt von Frankreich.

So beschreibst du, was jemand anhat:

Lily **is** wear**ing** green glasses.	Lily trägt eine grüne Brille.

▶ AH S. 64

Hören mit dem Hör-Profi

Der Hör-Profi hilft mir, Hörtexte und Gespräche zu verstehen.
Ich merke mir die Schritte 1–3 des Hör-Profis.
Ich wende den Hör-Profi bei Hörtexten und Videos an.
Auf diesen Seiten kann ich üben: 4, 10, 11, 20, 21, 23, 26, 30, 33, 40, 41, 44, 50, 53, 62 (Hörtexte); 8, 17, 36, 46, 56, 61 (Videos).

1 Vor dem Hören

Ich sehe mir die Bilder an.
Was sehe ich?
Was passiert?

Was kann ich auf Englisch sagen?

2 Beim Hören

Ich höre den Text einmal.
Welche Wörter verstehe ich?
Was sehe ich auch auf den Bildern?

Bei Videos:
Was sagen mir die Gesichter?
Was tun die Hände?

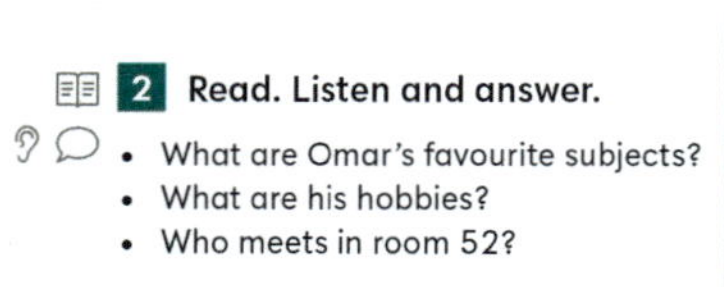

Ich lese die Fragen.
Worum geht es?
Was soll ich herausfinden?
Was verraten mir die Schlüsselwörter?

Ich höre den Text genau.
Was weiß ich jetzt?

3 Nach dem Hören

Ich beantworte die Fragen.

Ich überlege zum Schluss:
Was habe ich gut gemacht?
Was weiß ich jetzt?

Sprechen mit dem Sprech-Profi

Der Sprech-Profi hilft mir, deutlich und verständlich zu sprechen.
Ich merke mir die Schritte 1–3 des Sprech-Profis.
Ich wende den Sprech-Profi bei Sprech-Aufgaben an.
Auf diesen Seiten kann ich üben: 5, 6, 11, 12, 14, 21, 22, 23, 24, 27, 29, 31, 32, 34, 35, 39, 41, 42, 43, 44, 51, 52, 54, 55, 57, 60, 61, 62, 64.

1 Vor dem Sprechen

Ich höre das Wort oder den Satz mehrmals.
Wie klingt das Wort?
Wie klingt der Satz?

Ich spreche leise mit.

2 Beim Sprechen

Ich spreche das Wort oder den Satz laut nach.
Wie klingt das bei mir?

Ich lese und sage das Wort oder den Satz.
Ich schließe die Augen und wiederhole laut.

Ich übe so lange, bis ich das Wort oder den Satz sicher sagen kann.

3 Nach dem Sprechen

Ich verwende das Wort oder den Satz so oft wie möglich.
Wo kann ich das Wort verwenden?
Wo kann ich den Satz verwenden?
Welche anderen Sätze kann ich genauso bilden?

Ich überlege zum Schluss:
Was habe ich gut gemacht?
Welche Wörter oder Sätze will ich mir merken?

Lesen mit dem Lese-Profi

Der Lese-Profi hilft mir, Texte zu lesen und zu verstehen.
Ich merke mir die Schritte 1–3 des Lese-Profis.
Ich wende den Lese-Profi bei Texten an.
Auf diesen Seiten kann ich üben: 7, 13, 15, 16-17, 25, 27, 33, 37, 45, 47, 53, 55, 57, 62, 63.

1 Vor dem Lesen

Ich sehe mir die Bilder an.
Was sehe ich? Was passiert?

Ich lese die Überschrift.
Was könnte in dem Text stehen?

Ich sehe mir den ganzen Text an.
Was fällt mir auf? Gibt es hervorgehobene Wörter? Gibt es Abschnitte?

2 Beim Lesen

Ich lese den Text. Ich kann ihn mir auch anhören.
Welche Wörter verstehe ich?
Was sehe ich auch auf den Bildern?

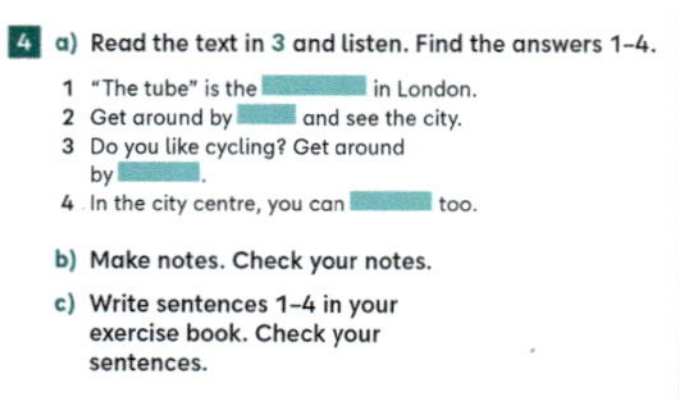
4 a) Read the text in 3 and listen. Find the answers 1–4.
1 "The tube" is the ___ in London.
2 Get around by ___ and see the city.
3 Do you like cycling? Get around by ___.
4 In the city centre, you can ___ too.

b) Make notes. Check your notes.
c) Write sentences 1–4 in your exercise book. Check your sentences.

Ich lese die Fragen.
Was soll ich herausfinden?
Was verraten mir die Schlüsselwörter?

Ich lese den Text genau.
Ich achte auf die Schlüsselwörter.
Was weiß ich jetzt?
Wenn ich einzelne Wörter nicht verstehe:
- Hilft mir der Satz?
- Kenne ich ähnliche Wörter in anderen Sprachen?
- Ich benutze eine Wörterbuch-App.

3 Nach dem Lesen

Ich beantworte die Fragen mündlich oder schriftlich.

Ich überlege zum Schluss:
Was habe ich gut gemacht?
Was nehme ich aus dem Text mit?

Schreiben mit dem Schreib-Profi

Der Schreib-Profi hilft mir, richtig und verständlich zu schreiben.
Ich merke mir die Schritte 1–3 des Schreib-Profis.
Ich wende den Schreib-Profi an, wenn ich Wörter, Sätze und Texte schreibe.
Auf diesen Seiten kann ich üben: 13, 14, 17, 19, 24, 28, 38, 39, 49, 52, 59, 61, 63.

My friend has **short brown hair**.
My friend has **green eyes**.
My friend is **helpful**.
He is **funny**.
He is good at **running**.
We **play football** and we **chill**.

1 Vor dem Schreiben

Ich sehe mir das Wort, den Satz oder den Text genau an.
Worauf muss ich besonders achten?
Gibt es hervorgehobene Wörter?
Wie ist der Satz oder der Text aufgebaut?

2 Beim Schreiben

Ich schreibe das Wort, den Satz oder den Text sorgfältig auf.
Ich nutze die Hilfen in meinem Schulbuch:
Die türkisblauen Wörter in den Muster-Sätzen sind Beispiele.
Ich ersetze die türkisblauen Wörter durch meine eigenen Ideen.
Ich benutze Hilfen wie die Wörterliste oder eine Wörterbuch-App.

3 Nach dem Schreiben

Ich überprüfe die Wörter, Buchstabe für Buchstabe.
Ich überprüfe die einzelnen Sätze und den ganzen Text.
Habe ich alles richtig geschrieben?
Kann ich alles lesen und verstehen?

Wenn ich einen Fehler finde, verbessere ich ihn.

My friend has long black hair.
My friend has brown eyes.
My frend is clever.
She is funi.

Wenn ich am PC schreibe, erkenne ich Fehler an den Wellenlinien unter den Wörtern.

Ich überlege zum Schluss:
Was habe ich gut gemacht?
Was kann ich jetzt?

Wörterliste

Wörter, die mit einem Kringel (°) markiert sind, gehören nicht zum Lernwortschatz.

A

a, an	ein, eine

Vor den Vokalen **a, e, i, o, u** *steht meist* **an** *statt* **a**:

a	an
a banana a tomato a new T-shirt	an apple an orange an old T-shirt

°a week	pro Woche
about	über
°account	der Account, das Konto
across	über *(quer über)*
active	aktiv
°activity	die Aktivität, die Tätigkeit
again	wieder, noch einmal
agree	zustimmen; einverstanden sein
°all	alle(s)
alone	allein
°always	immer
amazing	großartig, toll, erstaunlich
and	und
animal	das Tier
ankle	der Knöchel, das Fußgelenk
answer	(be)antworten
apple	der Apfel
April	der April
are: The books are £2.	Die Bücher kosten 2 Pfund.
are: they are	sie sind
aren't: they aren't	sie sind nicht
arm	der Arm
art	die Kunst
at 8 o'clock	um 8 Uhr
at home	zu Hause
at school	in der Schule
at the table	am Tisch
at the weekend	am Wochenende
°at Tower Bridge	auf/an der Tower Bridge
August	der August
aunt	die Tante
autumn	der Herbst

B

banana	die Banane
band	die Band
be	sein

Das Verb **be**

I **am** (= I'm)	*ich bin*
you **are** (= you're)	*du bist*
he/she/it **is** (= he's, she's, it's)	*er/sie/es ist*
we **are** (= we're)	*wir sind*
you **are** (= you're)	*ihr seid*
they **are** (they're)	*sie sind*

beach	der Strand
°beach clean-up	die Strandsäuberung
because	weil
bed	das Bett
best	beste, bester, bestes; am besten
best friend	der beste Freund, die beste Freundin
Best wishes	Viele Grüße *(Briefschluss)*
big	groß
bike	das Fahrrad
birthday	der Geburtstag
black	schwarz
blond	blond
blue	blau
board	die Tafel
body	der Körper

book	das Buch
boring	langweilig
boy	der Junge
braces *(Mehrzahl)*	die Zahnspange, die Zahnklammer
bread	das Brot
breakfast	das Frühstück
bridge	die Brücke
brother	der Bruder
brown	braun
bus	der Bus
°**bus stop**	die Bushaltestelle
but	aber
butter	die Butter
buy	kaufen
by bus	mit dem Bus
by card	mit der Karte *(Kreditkarte, Bankkarte)*

C

call	anrufen
°**camp**	das (Zelt-)Lager
can	können
Can you say that again, please?	Kannst du das bitte noch mal sagen?
candle	die Kerze
can't: I can't	ich kann nicht
cap	die (Schirm-)Mütze, die Kappe
capital	die Hauptstadt
car	das Auto
card	die Karte
caring	fürsorglich, liebevoll
cash	das Bargeld
°**castle**	die Burg
cat	die Katze
celebration	die Feier, das Fest
centre	das Zentrum; die Mitte
cereal	die Frühstücksflocken
chair	der Stuhl
chat (with)	chatten (mit); sich unterhalten (mit)

Wenn auf **chat** *eine Endung folgt, schreibt man das* **-t** *doppelt:* cha**tt**ing, cha**tt**ed

check	(über)prüfen, kontrollieren
cheese	der Käse
chicken	das Huhn; das Hähnchen
chill	chillen
chilling	das Chillen
chips *(Mehrzahl)*	die Pommes frites
cinema	das Kino
city	die (Groß-)Stadt
class	die Klasse; der Unterricht; der Kurs
clean	**1.** sauber **2.** sauber machen, putzen
clever	schlau, klug
close	schließen, zumachen
clothes *(Mehrzahl)*	die Kleidung, die Kleidungsstücke
cloudy	bewölkt, wolkig
cold	kalt

Englisch	*Deutsch*
It's cold. **It's** hot.	***Es ist*** *kalt.* ***Es ist*** *heiß.*
I'm cold. **I'm** hot.	***Mir ist*** *kalt.* ***Mir ist*** *heiß.*

colour	die Farbe
°**come**	(mit)kommen
comment	der Kommentar
communicative	kommunikativ, mitteilsam
computer	der Computer
computer game	das Computerspiel

Wörterliste

computing	die Informatik
cooking	das Kochen
cool	cool
corn	der Mais
cousin	der Cousin, die Cousine
creative	kreativ
cupboard	der Schrank
cushion	das Kissen
cycling	das Radfahren

D

dad	der Papa, der Vati
dancing	das Tanzen
°**darts**	das Darts, das Dartspiel
°**day**	der Tag
Dear ...	Liebe ..., Lieber ... (*Briefanfang, Begrüßung*)
December	der Dezember
degree	das Grad
Denmark	Dänemark
desk	der Schreibtisch
did *Vergangenheit von* **do**	machte(n), tat(en)
Did you see Lily?	Hast du Lily gesehen?
dinner	das Abendessen
dirty	schmutzig
do; *Vergangenheit* **did**	machen, tun; machte(n), tat(en)
do homework	die Hausaufgaben machen

Englisch: **Do** your homework.
Deutsch: **Mach** *deine Hausaufgaben.*

do my nails	meine Nägel machen
do sport	Sport machen / treiben
Do you like swimming?	Magst du Schwimmen?
do: What are you doing?	Was machst du (gerade)?
does: What does Lily eat?	Was isst Lily (gerne)?
doesn't: She doesn't eat ...	Sie isst nicht ..., Sie mag keine(n) ...

Kurzformen und Langformen:
doesn**'t** = does **not**
don**'t** = do **not**
didn**'t** = did **not**

dog	der Hund
door	die Tür
drawing	das Zeichnen
drink	**1.** das Getränk **2.** trinken

E

eat	essen
egg	das Ei
eleven	elf
email	die E-Mail
England	England
English	Englisch; englisch
Europe	Europa
every	jeder/jede/jedes
every Monday	jeden Montag
everybody	alle, jeder
°**excited**	aufgeregt
exciting	aufregend
Excuse me, ...	Entschuldigung, ... / Entschuldigen Sie, ...
exercise	die Übung, die Aufgabe
eye	das Auge

F

family	die Familie
father	der Vater
favourite	Lieblings-
February	der Februar
feel	fühlen; sich fühlen
finger	der Finger

first	erste(r, s)
fish; *Mehrzahl* **fish**	der Fisch; die Fische
fit	passen
folder	die Mappe, der Ordner
follow	*(online)* folgen
food	das Essen, das Lebensmittel
foot; *Mehrzahl* **feet**	der Fuß; die Füße
football	der Fußball
for	für
for breakfast	zum Frühstück
for homework	als Hausaufgabe
fourth (4th)	vierte(r, s)
France	Frankreich
free	**1.** frei **2.** kostenlos
Friday	der Freitag
friend	der Freund, die Freundin
friendly	freundlich, nett
from	von, aus
°**fun fact**	interessantes Detail; nebenbei bemerkt
funny	witzig, lustig

G

game	das Spiel
gaming	das Gaming *(das Spielen am Computer)*
garden centre	das Gartencenter; die Gärtnerei
gardening	das Gärtnern
German	Deutsch
Germany	Deutschland
get around	herumkommen
get (to)	(hin)kommen (nach, zu)
girl	das Mädchen
give	geben
glasses *(Mehrzahl)*	die Brille
glue stick	der Klebestift
go; *Vergangenheit* **went**	gehen, fahren; ging(en), fuhr(en)
go shopping	einkaufen gehen
go straight on	geradeaus gehen
good	gut
be good at sth.	etwas gut können; gut in etwas sein
Good idea!	Gute Idee!
Good morning.	Guten Morgen.
Good to see you.	Schön, dich zu sehen.
Goodbye.	Auf Wiedersehen.
grandfather	der Großvater
grandma	die Oma
grandmother	die Großmutter
grandpa	der Opa
great	toll
green	grün
guinea pig	das Meerschweinchen

H

had *Vergangenheit von* **have**	hatte(n)
hair	das Haar, die Haare
ham	der Schinken
hamster	der Hamster
hand	die Hand
happy	glücklich, froh
Happy birthday!	Herzlichen Glückwunsch zum Geburtstag!
hard-working	fleißig
has: he/she/it has	er/sie/es hat
have; *Vergangenheit* **had**	haben; hatte(n)
have dinner	(zu) Abend essen
he	er
head	der Kopf
hear	hören
Hello.	Hallo.
help	helfen

Wörterliste

helpful	hilfsbereit; hilfreich
her name is	sie heißt
°here	hier; hierher
Here you are.	Bitte schön. / Hier, bitte.
Hi.	Hallo. / Hi.
hiking	das Wandern
his name is	er heißt
history	die Geschichte *(das Schulfach)*
hobby; *Mehrzahl* **hobbies**	das Hobby; die Hobbys

Englisch: hobb**y** – hobb**ies**
Deutsch: das Hobby – die Hobbys

home	das Zuhause
homework	die Hausaufgabe(n)
honest	ehrlich
horse	das Pferd
hospital	das Krankenhaus
hot	heiß
How ...?	Wie ...?
How much is/are ...?	Was (Wie viel) kostet/ kosten ...?
How are you?	Wie geht's? / Wie geht es dir/euch?
How old are you?	Wie alt bist du?
hundred: a/one hundred	(ein)hundert
hurt	wehtun

I

ice tea	der Eistee
idea	die Idee
I'm (= I am)	ich bin
I'm fine.	Mir geht es gut.
I'm sorry.	Tut mir leid.
I'm taking photos.	Ich mache (gerade) Fotos.
important	wichtig
in	in
in spring	im Frühling
information	die Information(en)
is: The football is £3.	Der Fußball kostet 3 Pfund.
it	es
it's (= it is)	es ist *(bei Sachen und Tieren auch:* er ist; sie ist*)*
It's me.	Ich bin's.

J

jacket	die Jacke, das Jackett
jam	die Marmelade
January	der Januar

Die Monate schreibt man immer groß: **J**anuary, **F**ebruary, ...

jeans *(Mehrzahl)*	die Jeans
job	die Aufgabe; der Job, die (Arbeits-)Stelle
juice	der Saft
July	der Juli
June	der Juni

K

karate	Karate
°king	der König
knee	das Knie

Manche Buchstaben spricht man nicht aus:
knee („nii"), **h**onest („onest"),
san**d**wich („sänwitsch"), ...

L

lamp	die Lampe
last	letzte(r, s)
last weekend	letztes Wochenende
later	später
left	links
leg	das Bein

lemonade	die Limonade
lend	leihen
Let's ...	Lass(t) uns ...
like	mögen
I'd like a sandwich. (= I would like)	Ich hätte gern ein Sandwich.
I'd like to work at ...	Ich würde gerne in ... arbeiten.
lion	der Löwe
listen (to)	(sich etwas) anhören; zuhören
live	leben, wohnen
long	lang
Look!	Sieh mal!
look after my sister	auf meine Schwester aufpassen
look for	suchen
°**Look left/right!**	Schau nach links/rechts!
lots of	viel, viele
loud	laut
lunch	das Mittagessen

M

make	machen, herstellen
make dinner	Abendessen machen
March	der März
°**market**	der Markt
maths	die Mathe(matik)
May	der Mai
meet	kennenlernen; (sich) treffen
message	die Nachricht, die Mitteilung
milk	die Milch
Monday	der Montag

Die Wochentage schreibt man immer groß: **M**onday, **T**uesday, ...

monkey	der Affe
mother	die Mutter
mouse; *Mehrzahl* **mice**	die Maus; die Mäuse
Mr Lee	Herr Lee
Ms Bond	Frau Bond
mum	die Mama, die Mutti
museum	das Museum
mushroom	der Pilz, der Champignon
music	die Musik
my name is	ich heiße

N

nail	der Fingernagel
name	der Name
°**national park**	der Nationalpark
°**near**	nahe (bei), in der Nähe von
neighbour	der Nachbar, die Nachbarin
the Netherlands	die Niederlande
new	neu
next to	neben
nice	nett
Nice to meet you.	Schön, dich kennenzulernen.
no	nein
No, I don't. *(freundliche Kurzantwort)*	Nein.
No, I didn't.	Nein.

Auf die Frage **Do you like swimming?** *solltest du nicht nur mit yes oder no antworten. Die höfliche Antwort lautet* **No, I don't.** *oder* **Yes, I do.** *Die höfliche Antwort auf* **Did you go hiking?** *lautet* **No, I didn't**. *oder* **Yes, I did.**

not so	nicht so
November	der November
number	die Zahl, die Nummer

Wörterliste

O

o'clock: at 8 o'clock	um 8 Uhr
October	der Oktober
°**of**	von
OK	OK, in Ordnung
old	alt
on	auf
on Monday	am Montag
on the 4th of April	am vierten April
on the bus	im Bus
onion	die Zwiebel
online	online, Online-
open	öffnen; aufschlagen *(Buch)*
or	oder
orange	die Orange; orange(farben)
organizing	das Organisieren
°**our**	unser/e

P

page (= p.)	die (Buch-/Heft-)Seite
park	der Park
parrot	der Papagei
partner	der Partner, die Partnerin
party	die Party
pasta	die Pasta, die Nudeln
pay	zahlen, bezahlen
pay cash	bar bezahlen
pen	der Kugelschreiber, der Stift; der Füller
pencil	der Bleistift
pencil case	das Federmäppchen
people	die Leute, die Menschen
pepper	die Paprika
°**per day/hour**	pro Tag/Stunde
pet	das (Haus-)Tier
phone	das Handy, das Telefon
photo	das Foto
°**picture**	das Bild
pink	pink, rosa
pizza	die Pizza
place	der Ort, der Platz
°**plastic**	das Plastik, der Kunststoff
play	spielen
playing	das Spielen
please	bitte
°**point**	der Punkt
Poland	Polen
positive	positiv
post	**1.** posten *(im Internet veröffentlichen)* °**2.** der Post
pound (£)	das Pfund *(britische Währung)*

Man schreibt:	*Man sagt:*
£ 1	one **pound**
£ 2.50	two **pounds** fifty
90 p	ninety pence (auch „pii“)

present	das Geschenk
problem	das Problem

Q

quiet	ruhig, still, leise

R

rabbit	das Kaninchen
rainy	regnerisch
rat	die Ratte
red	rot
relaxed	entspannt, locker
reliable	verlässlich, zuverlässig
restaurant	das Restaurant
right	rechts
°**river**	der Fluss
roll	das Brötchen

room	der Raum, das Zimmer
rubber	der/das Radiergummi
rucksack	der Rucksack
°**rugby**	das Rugby *(Ballsportart)*
ruler	das Lineal
running	das Laufen, das Rennen

S

°**sad**	traurig
salad	der Salat *(als Gericht oder Beilage)*
sandwich	das Sandwich
Saturday	der Samstag, der Sonnabend
sausage	das Würstchen, die Wurst
say (about)	sagen (über)
school	die Schule
school things	die Schulsachen
science	die Naturwissenschaft *(auch als Schulfach)*
second (2nd)	zweite(r, s)
see	sehen
See you. / See you later.	Bis dann. / Bis später.
September	der September
series	die Serie, die Sendereihe
she	sie
shelf; *Mehrzahl* **shelves**	das Regal(brett); die Regale, das Regal *(mit mehreren Brettern)*
shoe	der Schuh
shop	das Geschäft, der Laden
shop assistant	der Verkäufer, die Verkäuferin
shopping	das Einkaufen; die Einkäufe
short	kurz
shorts *(Mehrzahl)*	die kurze Hose, die Shorts
should: A good friend should ...	Ein guter Freund / Eine gute Freundin sollte ...
sick	krank
sight	die Sehenswürdigkeit
sister	die Schwester
sit	sitzen; sich setzen
skatepark	der Skatepark
skirt	der Rock
small	klein
snake	die Schlange
snowy	scheebedeckt, verschneit
°**social media**	die sozialen Medien
°**social worker**	der Sozialarbeiter, die Sozialarbeiterin
sock	die Socke
sofa	das Sofa
some	einige, ein paar; etwas, ein wenig

Some *verwendet man*
1. *wenn man etwas nicht zählen kann:*
   some lemonade, **some** ice tea
2. *wenn man nicht weiß, wie viele es sind:*
   some tomatoes

souvenir	das Souvenir
sport	der Sport; die Sportart
sports field	der Sportplatz, das Sportfeld
spring	der Frühling
°**stadium**	das Stadion
stomach	der Bauch
straight on	geradeaus (weiter)
street	die Straße
°**street art**	die Straßenkunst
stressful	stressig
strong point	die Stärke; die starke Seite
student	der Schüler, die Schülerin; der Student, die Studentin
subject	das (Schul-)Fach
summer	der Sommer
Sunday	der Sonntag

Wörterliste

sunny	sonnig
supermarket	der Supermarkt
surfing	das Surfing
sweatshirt	das Sweatshirt
swimming	das Schwimmen
swimming pool	das Schwimmbad

T

table	der Tisch
table tennis	das Tischtennis
tablet	das Tablet, der Tabletcomputer
take photos	Fotos machen
takeaway	die Imbissbude
talk (about)	sprechen, reden (über)
talk to	sprechen, reden mit
tea	der Tee
teacher	der Lehrer, die Lehrerin
team	das Team, die Mannschaft
Tell me about ...	Erzähle mir von ...
thank you	danke (schön)
thanks	danke
that	das (dort)
that's (= that is)	das (da) ist
°That's right.	Das ist richtig.
°That's wrong.	Das ist falsch.
the	der, die, das

Den Artikel **the** *spricht man unterschiedlich aus:*
1. *Vor Konsonanten wie „thä“:*
   the chips, **the h**am, **the p**izza
2. *Vor Vokalen meist wie “thii“:*
   the ice tea, **the o**range

Im Englischen spricht man den Laut “th” besonders aus. Höre dir folgende Wörter in einer Wörterbuch-App an: **th**anks, **th**ing, **th**ird *und* **th**e, **th**en, **th**ey.

then	dann, danach
there	dort, dorthin
there are	es gibt
there is	es gibt

So sagst du ***„Es gibt ...“*** *auf Englisch:*
Einzahl: **There is** 1 chair.
Mehrzahl: **There are** 2 chairs.

they are	sie sind
they aren't (= are not)	sie sind nicht
thing	das Ding, die Sache
think	denken, finden
think: I think ...	Ich denke/finde, ...
third (3rd)	dritte(r, s)
thirteen	dreizehn (13)
This is Zane.	Das ist Zane.
Thursday	der Donnerstag
ticket	die Eintrittskarte, die Fahrkarte, das Ticket
time	die Zeit; die Uhrzeit
°tip	der Tipp
tired	müde
to the board	an die Tafel
today	heute
°together	zusammen
tomato; *Mehrzahl* **tomatoes**	die Tomate; die Tomaten
too	auch
too small	zu klein
tooth; *Mehrzahl* **teeth**	der Zahn; die Zähne
°tourist	der/die Tourist/in
°tourist information	die Touristeninformation
town	die Stadt
train	der Zug, die Eisenbahn
°transport	das Fortbewegungsmittel
trousers *(Mehrzahl)*	die Hose
°tube (the tube)	die Londoner U-Bahn
Tuesday	der Dienstag
tuna	der Thunfisch

turn right/left	(nach) rechts/links abbiegen
twenty-fifth (25th)	fünfundzwanzigste(r, s)

U

uncle	der Onkel
under	unter
underground	die U-Bahn
understand	verstehen
the United Kingdom (the UK)	das Vereinigte Königreich

V

veggie spread	der vegetarische Aufstrich
very	sehr
video	das Video
visit	besuchen

W

walk	(zu Fuß) gehen, wandern
walk the dog	mit dem Hund spazieren gehen, Gassi gehen
wardrobe	der Kleiderschrank
warm	warm
watch	(sich etwas) anschauen
water	das Wasser
we	wir
wear	tragen, anhaben *(Kleidung)*
weather	das Wetter
Wednesday	der Mittwoch
week	die Woche
weekend	das Wochenende
Welcome (back)!	Willkommen (zurück)!
went *Vergangenheit von* **go**	ging(en), fuhr(en)
What ...?	Was ...?
What about you?	Und du? / Was ist mit dir?
What are your strong points?	Was sind deine Stärken?
What would you like for Christmas?	Was wünschst du dir zu Weihnachten?
What's your favourite animal?	Was ist dein Lieblingstier?
°**What's for dinner?**	Was gibt's zum Abendessen?
What's the time?	Wie spät ist es?
What's ... like?	Wie ist ...? / Wie sieht ... aus?
What's your name?	Wie heißt du? (*wörtlich:* Was ist dein Name?)

What's *ist die Kurzform von* **What is**.

When ...?	Wann ...?
When is your birthday?	Wann hast du Geburtstag?
Where ...?	Wo ...?
Where would you like to work?	Wo würdest du gerne arbeiten?
white	weiß
°**Who ...?**	Wer ...?
Why ...?	Warum ...?
window	das Fenster
windy	windig
winter	der Winter
with	mit
word	das Wort
work	arbeiten
Would you like ...?	Möchtest du ...?
write	schreiben

Y

°**year**	das Jahr
yellow	gelb
yes	ja

Yes, I do. *(freundliche Kurzantwort)*	Ja.
Yes, I did. *(freundliche Kurzantwort)*	Ja.
yoghurt	der/das Joghurt
you	du; dich; dir; ihr; euch; Sie; Ihnen
your	dein, deine; euer; Ihr; ihr
you're (= you are)	du bist; ihr seid; Sie sind
You're welcome.	Bitte, gern geschehen. / Nichts zu danken.
youth centre	das Jugendzentrum

Let's talk

Classroom English

Du kannst dir die Sätze in der App anhören.

▶ Hilfe

You and your teacher	Du und dein Lehrer / deine Lehrerin
Good morning, Mr / Ms ...	Guten Morgen, Herr / Frau ...
Can I close / open the window, please?	Kann ich bitte das Fenster zumachen / aufmachen?
Can I go to the board?	Kann ich an die Tafel gehen?
Can we listen to a song?	Können wir ein Lied anhören?
Can we play a game?	Können wir ein Spiel spielen?
Can we watch a video?	Können wir ein Video anschauen?
Goodbye.	Auf Wiedersehen.
What's for homework?	Was haben wir als Hausaufgabe auf?

What your teacher says	Was dein Lehrer / deine Lehrerin sagt
Be quiet, please.	Sei bitte leise. / Seid bitte leise.
Check your answers.	Überprüft eure Antworten / Ergebnisse.
Do exercise 3 for homework.	Macht Übung 3 als Hausaufgabe.
Go to the board, please.	Geh bitte an die Tafel.
Let's do exercise 3.	Lasst uns Übung 3 machen.
Listen, please.	Hör bitte zu. / Hört bitte zu.
Open your books on page 8.	Schlagt Seite 8 auf.
Make notes.	Mache dir Notizen. / Macht euch Notizen.
Practise with a partner.	Übt zu zweit.
Say it again, please.	Sag das bitte noch mal.
Say it in German / English, please.	Sag es bitte auf Deutsch / Englisch.
Write the words / sentences in your exercise books.	Schreibt die Wörter / die Sätze in euer Heft.

You need help	Du brauchst Hilfe
Can you help me, please?	Können Sie mir bitte helfen? / Kannst du mir bitte helfen?
Can you say that again, please?	Können Sie das bitte noch einmal sagen? / Kannst du das bitte noch einmal sagen?
I don't understand.	Ich habe das nicht verstanden.
What's *Lineal* in English?	Was heißt „Lineal" auf Englisch?
What's „pen" in German?	Was heißt *pen* auf Deutsch?
What page, please?	Welche Seite, bitte?

Let's talk

Classroom English

Du kannst dir die Sätze in der App anhören.

▶ Hilfe

Work with a partner / Work in a group	Zu zweit arbeiten / In einer Gruppe arbeiten
Can I work with Ella (and Luca)?	Kann ich mit Ella (und Luca) arbeiten?
Can I have your pen, please?	Kann ich bitte deinen Stift haben?
Yes, you can. Here you are.	Ja. Hier, bitte.
No, you can't. I'm sorry.	Nein. Tut mir leid.
Thanks, Rico.	Danke, Rico.
You're welcome.	Gern geschehen.

Give your opinion	Deine Meinung sagen
I think ...	Ich denke / finde, ...
I don't think ...	Ich denke / finde nicht, ...
I agree.	Ich stimme (dir) zu.
Sorry, I don't agree.	Tut mir leid. Ich stimme (dir) nicht zu.
That's very important.	Das ist sehr wichtig.
That's not (so) important.	Das ist nicht (so) wichtig.

Give feedback	Feedback geben
Good work!	Gute Arbeit! Gut gemacht!
Good eye contact!	Guter Blickkontakt!
I like your ideas. I like your poster / ...	Mir gefallen deine Ideen. Mir gefällt dein Plakat / ...
Your poster / ... is cool / very creative.	Dein Plakat / ... ist cool / sehr kreativ.
Your pictures are good / great.	Deine Bilder sind gut / toll.
You spoke loudly and clearly.	Du hast laut und deutlich gesprochen.
You made pauses.	Du hast Pausen gemacht.

Numbers

Du kannst dir die Grundzahlen 1 bis 100 in der App anhören. ▶ Hilfe

1	one
2	two
3	three
4	four
5	five
6	six
7	seven
8	eight
9	nine
10	ten
11	eleven
12	twelve
13	thirteen
14	fourteen
15	fifteen
16	sixteen
17	seventeen
18	eighteen
19	nineteen

20	twenty
21	twenty-one
22	twenty-two
23	twenty-three
24	twenty-four
25	twenty-five
26	twenty-six
27	twenty-seven
28	twenty-eight
29	twenty-nine
30	thirty
40	forty
50	fifty
60	sixty
70	seventy
80	eighty
90	ninety
100	one hundred / a hundred

Du kannst dir die Ordnungszahlen 1. bis 31. in der App anhören. ▶ Hilfe

1st	first
2nd	second
3rd	third
4th	fourth
5th	fifth
6th	sixth
7th	seventh
8th	eighth
9th	ninth
10th	tenth
11th	eleventh
12th	twelfth
13th	thirteenth
14th	fourteenth
15th	fifteenth
16th	sixteenth

17th	seventeenth
18th	eighteenth
19th	nineteenth
20th	twentieth
21st	twenty-first
22nd	twenty-second
23rd	twenty-third
24th	twenty-fourth
25th	twenty-fifth
26th	twenty-sixth
27th	twenty-seventh
28th	twenty-eighth
29th	twenty-ninth
30th	thirtieth
31st	thirty-first

Quellenverzeichnis

Cover
Cornelsen/Nils Fliegner

Illustrationen
Cornelsen/Carl Pearce (Beehive Illustration Agency): S. 7/o.l., S. 7/o.r., S. 7/u.l., S. 7/u.r., S. 15/M.l., S. 15/M.r., S. 15/o.l., S. 15/o.M., S. 15/o.r., S. 27, S. 37, S. 47/M.l., S. 47/M.M., S. 47/u.M., S. 47/u.r., S. 57; Cornelsen/Joseph Wilkins (Beehive Illustration Agency): S. 3/v.o.n.u. 2, S. 3/v.o.n.u. 3, S. 3/v.o.n.u. 4, S. 3/v.o.n.u. 5, S. 3/v.o.n.u. 6, S. 5/u.l., S. 5/u.r., S. 6, S. 9, S. 10, S. 11/Illustrationen, S. 12, S. 14, S. 15/u.r., S. 20, S. 21/Illustrationen, S. 22/o., S. 22/u., S. 23, S. 24, S. 29/Illustrationen, S. 30, S. 31, S. 32, S. 33/M.u.r., S. 33/u.r., S. 34, S. 35/u.l., S. 35/u.r., S. 38, S. 39, S. 40, S. 41, S. 42, S. 43, S. 44/o., S. 49/u.l., S. 49/u.r., S. 50, S. 51, S. 52, S. 53/o.l., S. 53/o.M., S. 53/o.r., S. 54, S. 58, S. 59/M.l., S. 59/M.r., S. 59/u., S. 60/Illustrationen, S. 62/o., S. 63, S. 64/Illustrationen, S. 66/o., S. 81, S. 82; Cornelsen/Nils Fliegner: S. 1

Fotos
S. 3/v.o.n.u. 1: Shutterstock.com/Globe Turner; S. 3/v.o.n.u. 7: Shutterstock.com/yexelA; S. 4/o.l.: mauritius images/Steve Vidler; S. 4/o.r.: mauritius images/Stephen Olner/Alamy; S. 4/u.l.: mauritius images/Iain Sarjeant/Alamy; S. 4/u.r.: mauritius images/Loop Images; S. 5/o.l.: Cornelsen/Anja Poehlmann; S. 5/o.M.l.: Cornelsen/Chocolate Films; S. 5/o.M.r.: Cornelsen/Chocolate Films; S. 5/o.r.: Cornelsen/Chocolate Films; S. 7/Emojis: Shutterstock.com/Hussain Kazim; S. 8/Karte: stock.adobe.com/lesniewski; S. 8/Karte: Flaggen: Shutterstock.com/SLdesign; S. 8/Kompass: Shutterstock.com/languste; S. 8/u.r.: Shutterstock.com/Globe Turner; S. 11/u.: Shutterstock.com/manorm; S. 13/o.l.: mauritius images/Steve Vidler; S. 13/o.r.: Shutterstock.com/S-F; S. 13/u.l.: Shutterstock.com/r.nagy; S. 13/u.r.: mauritius images/dani codina/Alamy; S. 16/Emojis: Shutterstock.com/Hussain Kazim; S. 16/Katze: Shutterstock.com/Faisol Farhan; S. 16/M.o.: stock.adobe.com/Nicola; S. 16/M.u.: mauritius images/Novarc Images; S. 16/o.: Cornelsen, Hintergrund: stock.adobe.com/Photocreo Bednarek, Junge:; S. 16/Stadion: Shutterstock.com/Faisol Farhan; S. 16/u.: mauritius images/Michael Weber; S. 19/Hand: Shutterstock.com/Cali6ro; S. 19/o.l.: Shutterstock.com/Eszter Szadeczky-Kardoss; S. 19/o.r.: stock.adobe.com/Nicola; S. 19/u.r.: mauritius images/Novarc Images; S. 21/u.l.: Shutterstock.com/wavebreakmedia; S. 21/u.M.l.: Shutterstock.com/Monkey Business Images; S. 21/u.M.r.: stock.adobe.com/alexbrylovhk; S. 21/u.r.: Shutterstock.com/Oskari Porkka; S. 22/Emojis: Shutterstock.com/Hussain Kazim; S. 25/o.l.: Shutterstock.com/TeddyandMia; S. 25/o.M.: Shutterstock.com/HappyPictures; S. 25/o.r.: Shutterstock.com/svetlatek; S. 26/M.l.: mauritius images/Cody Froggatt/Alamy; S. 26/M.r.: mauritius images/Nigel Waldron/Alamy; S. 26/o.l.: stock.adobe.com/Kaspars; S. 26/o.r.: Cornelsen/Chocolate Films; S. 26/u.r.: mauritius images/News Images LTD/Alamy; S. 29/o.: Cornelsen/Gunnar Rossow; S. 33/Flagge: Shutterstock.com/Basthamp; S. 33/Haken: Shutterstock.com/Titov Nikolai; S. 33/Hände: Shutterstock.com/Michiru13; S. 33/Kreuz: Shutterstock.com/Titov Nikolai; S. 33/M.o.r. Strand: Shutterstock.com/Maryshot; S. 33/M.u.l. Strand: Shutterstock.com/VH-studio; S. 33/Papierkorb: Shutterstock.com/AlipFir; S. 35/Karte: Karte: Cornelsen/Joseph Wilkins (Beehive Illustration Agency); Tasche: Shutterstock.com/Ahmad Arzaha; Cafe: Shutterstock.com/VikiVector; Strand, Schwimmbad: Shutterstock.com/Mariia Lov; Bus: Shutterstock.com/NAPISAH NAPISAH; Brücke: Shutterstock.com/Alex Leo; Info: Shutterstock.com/viktor vorobyev; You are Here: Shutterstock.com/Alex.4L; S. 35/Pfeile: Shutterstock.com/QuirkCraft Studio; S. 36/o.l.: mauritius images/Destinations; S. 36/o.r.: stock.adobe.com/Apostolis Giontzis; S. 36/u.l.: mauritius images/Mike McEnnerney/Alamy; S. 36/u.r.: mauritius images/Paul Christian Gordon/Alamy; S. 44/u.l.: Cornelsen/Chocolate Films; S. 44/u.r.: Cornelsen/Chocolate Films; S. 45/1: Shutterstock.com/Nuwirana; S. 45/2: Shutterstock.com/Xeyal Yaqubov; S. 45/3: Shutterstock.com/nkrumah frederick; S. 45/4: Shutterstock.com/diosugiharto; S. 45/5: Shutterstock.com/Fourleaflover; S. 45/6: Shutterstock.com/Macro Icon; S. 45/u.M.: Shutterstock.com/Giuseppe_R; S. 46/M.r.: stock.adobe.com/wavebreak3; S. 46/u.r.: Shutterstock.com/David Pimborough; S. 46/o.l.: Shutterstock.com/Dilchaspiyaan; S.46/o.r.: stock.adobe.com/Tomas Marek; S.46/M.l.: stock.adobe.com/postywood1; S.47/M.r.: Cornelsen/Person re.: Chocolate Films, Wagen + Hintergrund: mauritius images/PHILIP SMITH/Alamy; S47/u.l.: Hintergrund: Shutterstock.com/1000 Words; Person: Cornelsen/Chocolate Films; Auto: mauritius images/PHILIP SMITH/Alamy; S. 49/Emojis: Shutterstock.com/Hussain Kazim; S. 53/Flaggen: Shutterstock.com/Globe Turner; S. 55/M.: Shutterstock.com/melitas; S. 55/u.l.: Cornelsen/Gunnar Rossow; S. 56/M.l.: mauritius images/Gerry Morgan/Alamy; S. 56/M.r.: mauritius images/Rene Mattes; S. 56/o.l.: mauritius images/Liam Cleary; S. 56/o.r.: stock.adobe.com/Patryk Kosmider; S. 56/u.r.: stock.adobe.com/Peter Hermes Furian; S. 59/o.l., o.r.: Shutterstock.com/LEA DINH; S. 59/o.r.: M.: Shutterstock.com/craftlove; S. 59/o.r.: o.: Shutterstock.com/Pixel-Shot; S. 59/o.r.: u.l.: Shutterstock.com/Bibadash; S. 59/o.r.: u.M.: Shutterstock.com/MURRIRA; S. 59/o.r.: u.r.: Shutterstock.com/melitas; S. 59/u.l.: Shutterstock.com/LEA DINH; S. 60/1. l.: Shutterstock.com/yexelA; S. 60/1. r.: Shutterstock.com/Vikusandra; S. 61/M.: Shutterstock.com/M.KOS; S. 61/o.r.: Shutterstock.com/ps-42; S. 62/u.: imago sport/Action Plus; S. 64/u.: mauritius images/Radharc Images/Alamy; S. 77: Shutterstock.com/Filatova Halyna; S. 86/Karte: Depositphotos/Iryna Volina; S. 86/Kompass: Shutterstock.com/languste

Texte
S. 53/1982+85 by Warn. Bros.Music Corp/New Hidden Valley. Music/C.B.-S. Music, NEUE WELT MV GMBH, Hamburg. Text: Burt Bacharach / Carole Bayer-Sager

EUROPE

Du kannst dir die Ländernamen in der App anhören.

▶ Hilfe

Albania	Czechia	Italy	Montenegro	Slovakia
Andorra	Denmark	Kazakhstan	the Netherlands	Slovenia
Armenia	Estonia	Kosovo	North Macedonia	Spain
Austria	Finland	Latvia	Norway	Sweden
Belarus	France	Liechtenstein	Poland	Switzerland
Belgium	Georgia	Lithuania	Portugal	Turkey
Bosnia-	Germany	Luxembourg	Romania	Ukraine
Herzegovina	Greece	Malta	Russia	the United Kingdom
Bulgaria	Hungary	Moldova	San Marino	(the UK)
Croatia	Iceland	Monaco	Serbia	Vatican City
Cyprus	Ireland			